THE LAST OF THE WHITE GUYS

Barclay Bates

Bloomsbury Press
San Francisco

Copyright 1999 by Barclay Bates

Published by Bloomsbury Press
P.O.Box 22395
San Francisco, CA 94122.

This is a work of fiction. Its characters and events proceed from the author's imagination, not real life. Any resemblance of characters to actual people living or dead is purely coincidental.

Bates, Barclay

The Last of the White Guys: a novel/by Barclay Bates
p.   cm.
ISBN 0-9667039-9-5
I Title
813'.54—dc21
Library of Congress Catalog Card Number: 98-74017

First Edition

To Tillie Olsen

And the memory of Arthur Foff

THE LAST

OF THE

WHITE GUYS

ONE

Though the sky was darkening, Bradford decided to fly the Stars and Stripes. From the engineer's room on the side alley he carried the flag out front, ran it up briskly, then lowered it to half-mast in honor of two consular employees machine-gunned the day before in Yemen. These days the flag was often at half-mast, last week for a policeman murdered in the Mission, today for the unlucky bureaucrats.

When he entered the main corridor, running late now, the sight of a cardboard box alarmed him. In the distance it sat in front of the Counseling Center, its squareness spoiling the clean, converging lines of floor and walls, its dull brown marring the polished tile. Bomb scare.

"Motherfucker!"

He spoke loudly, daring anyone to be there and hear. It sometimes comforted him to do private and outrageous things in this place. Once, alone in his office late at night, overworked and angry, he had masturbated into a silk blouse from the girls' lost-and-found box; but this morning no obscenity could help. If he had to call the cops, it would be noon before he and Shabazz could start work with

1

the kids, six before they would finish. So he was relieved to find no tape on the box, to see that the flaps had simply been folded shut, half of each holding down half of another. He nudged the thing with his toe and decided it was too light for a bomb. He studied it for another ten seconds and also decided that, since there was no sound or sight of movement within, it almost certainly did not contain snakes, of which he had a ubiquitous and abnormal fear. At last he bent down, plucked open the flaps. Inside was a plastic bag neatly tied with one of those paper-coated pieces of wire provided in the produce departments of grocery stores. The plastic was crinkled and dirty, and the light was not good, so Bradford had to squat and hunch forward before he could see into the cloudy interior.

Recognition made him flinch and shiver. The bag contained a small dead dog, lying on its side, its eyes open and glazed in what would have been, in a human, an expression of intense thoughtfulness. In color it was white or light gray, save for a darkness about the throat. Bending still closer, he saw that the darkness was a substance, presumably blood.

"Shit."

Bradford carried the box down the hall to the janitor's closet, locked it inside. Walking back, it occurred to him that this was the sort of event that people who were not high school administrators found first implausible and then rather frightening. It was really neither. All sorts of unpleasant things were left in schools, used condoms, excrement, buckets of dirty oil, live raccoons. From his office he called Animal Control and left a message on their machine. At last he turned on the lights and headed for the back entrance to admit his helpers from the Honor Society. Through glass reinforced by chicken wire, he made a second and happier discovery, not unexpected, one which caused a sharp pulse of excitement in each thigh and made him walk faster. Molly Marcus, captain of the girls' basketball team, a head taller than any of the others.

"Enter." Bradford bowed slightly. "O indispensable ones."

There were giggles as he shut the door on the mob outside. Molly Marcus, who did not giggle, said that flattery would get him nowhere.

And Jesus, she was wearing that skirt. He raised his chin and closed his eyes to keep from staring. Molly would graduate in June, and through Bradford swept the tenuous hope that, her demurral notwithstanding, flattery might eventually get him somewhere.

The kids gathered around.

"Behind every great assistant principal stand even greater student helpers."

Bradford paused for more giggles. Molly groaned. She had a baby face, fine brassy hair which fell nearly to her waist, small green eyes, and, depending on the precise degree of arch to her eyebrow, a wry or flatly distrusting look.

He assigned some kids to man the front door, others to monitor an orderly line in the foyer and hallway. Then he led the two senior girls into the Counseling Center, a large rectangular room. Around its perimeter was a series of small offices; before each, forming an inner rectangle, were two or three student desks. Bradford dragged a couple of them into the center of the room, glancing sideways at Molly, estimating the paltry distance between hem and underpants.

"You guys sit here."

He went into his office and sat down. Within seconds the first over-the-counters came through the doors. Thirteen Chinese, three Filipinos, one Latina, three Causcasians, one indeterminate. Irritation raced through him, born by caffeine. There was really no room for these kids. The enrollment was much too large as it was. But Molly and Grace intercepted them, seated them in order of arrival, and sent the first into Bradford's cubicle before he was quite ready. Alexander Hamilton had fewer clerks and administrators than any high school in the city simply because the kids could and did do so much of the donkey work.

Bradford shuffled papers, stalling, waiting to see where and how Molly would sit down. Molly Marcus did not often wear short skirts--preferring Levis, as did her peers; but she had the legs and ass of a movie queen. During sixth period the year before, she had fulfilled her Community Service Requirement by writing hall passes at a tiny table in the corner of Bradford's office. Four times she had arrived in the black garment she now wore, and on each occasion for fifty maddening minutes had displayed to him her long, bare perfect thighs and a triangle of white panties. Bradford had spent too much of this time imagining intensely the silkiness of the nylon; the soft fuzz of the cotton lining, slightly stained, probably with pee but perhaps with the juices of her random excitements; the warm dry thicket of coiling pubic hair; and at last the moist, pearl-colored paradise of her vagina.

When her term of servitude was over, Bradford missed the dazzling sight of her nether parts as much as he had missed anything in his life, and now he hoped for a reprise. But Molly had moved the desk, set it at an angle; and when she sat down displayed the exquisite thighs but not the holy place. He wanted to believe that she was torturing him deliberately; but could not. He was just another older guy; and she valued him only for the familiarity, the teasing, that he permitted. He supposed it gave her status among her peers.

Before starting work he looked at his watch. Forty minutes later he checked it again and did arithmetic in his head. He was programming one student every 5.3 minutes.

4

Bradford signaled to Molly to hold the next kid, then pulled the phone book from his drawer and made a perfunctory search. He found it difficult to believe that the name Rwanda Shabazz was in any phone book anywhere, and certainly it was not in his. He hit the predial number of Gordon Wong, Principal of Alexander Hamilton.

"Wong residence."

"Mickey, Gordon. Rwanda hasn't shown up, and I've got a hundred kids in line."

"Í know, I know. She leave message on my machine."

"Where is she?"

"I dunno. I can' unnerstan'. She soun' frantic."

"So what else is new."

"I be there half hour, max."

By the time Gordon showed up Bradford had programmed seven more kids.

"Still not here?"

"Do you see her."

"No. On tape, she say something about King? Who's King?"

"Gordon, with regard to Rwanda's private life, I am not *au courant*."

"Uh. I get to work."

"Blessings on you," said Bradford, enjoying the boss' look of mystification. Gordon was an energetic, decent, and reasonably intelligent man; but he had immigrated to the United States in his mid-teens, and his difficulties with the language were so great that a certain percentage of the time he did not understand what was going on around him. Bradford was uncertain about the precise figure. Fifteen percent, perhaps twenty. He had once told Janie Wetherall that when the affirmative action Tsunami had swamped the West Coast, Gordon had said a prayer, hung ten, and landed on the beach at Hamilton.

5

Gordon set up shop in the cubicle directly across the room, and for a time Bradford amused himself by comparing their speeds. But his incontestable superiority bored him, and soon he was watching Molly again. She did not have quite enough to do and often rose to pace or stretch or go to the water fountain in the hallway. Each time her lovely hip seemed to nudge the front of her desk a centimeter or two in Bradford's direction, ever closer to crotch-shot territory.

In an interval between customers, three new arrivals caught his attention. He stared at them. They did not look at him. When they were seated, he continued staring for perhaps ten seconds, as if hoping they would realize their mistake and leave. At last he got up, went outside, and approached Leticia Henderson, the one for whom he felt no actual dislike.

"What can I do for you?"

She handed him seemingly identical pieces of paper, stapled together. On top was a certificate of assignment made out at the Central Office. Bradford read it, flipped it over, and looked at the other, the one he himself had prepared and signed a few days earlier. Across its face in a large staggering script was "Cancelled—J. T. Alomar."

Bradford looked at the other kids, Oddibe Johnson and then Rickey Bradford. Rickey Bradford had disproportionately small features centered in a wide, square, sullen face. His shoulders were broad but thin and rounded. For these and more important reasons, Bradford detested sharing his name with the boy.

"You guys have these too?"

They nodded, but still wouldn't look at him. Bradford took a deep breath. His mind went blank for a moment. He went back into his office, checked his Rolodex for the number of Fats Morrell.

"Hello?"

"Mick Bradford, Fats."

"Yes."

"I'm at school, doing over-the-counters. On Wednesday I dropped three kids for academic failure, strictly according to procedure. Now they're in my office, and Alomar's cancelled the transfers. What's goin' on?"

"A Miz Henderson and some others."

"Right."

"The boss feels we oughta cut 'em some slack. Your black enrollment's down again, you know."

"Bradford is <u>white</u>, for Chrissake."

"Well, we really don't like to discriminate against you people."

"Ho, ho. Look, the rules call for one semester of probation. Each of these turkeys got two. I call that plenty of slack, and if they flunk any more classes, they don't graduate. All of 'em have a much better shot in a comprehensive school."

"I agree. But their folks have been appraised of the facts, and they still want 'em back at Hamilton."

"They're crazy."

"Face it, my man. It's what you get for having such a great reputation."

"Look. Rickey Bradford is a dealer. I can't prove it yet, but I know he is. What I don't know is how many ninth-grade teeny-boppers he's managing to turn on."

"Get the goods on him, and I'll sign the transfer myself. That's a commitment."

"What goods? A corpse?"

This was below the belt, and Bradford knew it.

After a moment Morrell said, "Sorry, Mick. Nothin' I can do."

Bradford hung up, dried his hands on his pantslegs, and took deep breaths to compose himself. At work he handled most challenges with equanimity, but drug dealers engendered rage and panic. The three newcomers were watching him now, and they were just smart enough to figure out what he'd been doing. Bradford rose, consciously relaxing the muscles of his face, trying to look merely surprised, He crossed the larger room, leaned into Gordon's cubicle, one hand on the doorframe.

"I've got some re-admits out here. The three on the end. You deal with 'em, okay?"

"If you wan'. Why?"

"Because I might fucking strangle one of them."

Gordon raised his hands, palms out. "Okay, okay."

Molly was waiting in Bradford's office. She handed him a piece of paper.

"This kid's from out of state. All he's got is this letter from the principal of his last school."

Bradford glanced at the paper, seeing nothing. "That's okay. Just put him in line."

"Your hands are shaking."

Bradford could not look at her. "That is correct."

His next customer was a tall and thin Chinese boy— Fresh Off the Boat, his second generation peers would say. He wore a pale green windbreaker, nondescript gray pants, blue sneakers from Penney's or Walgreen's. His hair was spikey and dull brown; it looked as if someone had set the clippers at one inch, then mowed his skull. He sat on the edge of his chair, spine straight, leaning toward Bradford with eyes as wide as those of Asian kids can possibly be. Bradford found the boy's transcript, stared at it, set it aside. As he took the transfer certificate, he realized he hadn't checked the grades to be sure the kid was eligible. Suddenly he didn't care.

"Okay. You're a junior, huh?"

"No! Soph-o-more!"

"Oh. Okay."

On a white program form Bradford wrote the boy's name and registry, then some courses.

"U. S. History required for soph-o-mores?"

Bradford read what he'd written. U. S. and English 5. Junior courses.

"No. It isn't," he said. "Sorry."

He tore up the card, furious—though of course the boy was just taking care of business, reading upside down, being sure the *lo fan* didn't screw him up. Like most Chinese kids, he asked if he could take Honors English, and Bradford delivered one of his Recorded Messages.

"Only those who score at the ninety-sixth percentile in total reading on the CTBS may enroll in Honors English. Your scores won't arrive until mid-semester. At that time you can see your counselor and find out if you're eligible to take Honors in the spring."

"What kind of test?"

"A standard achievement test. Everybody takes it."

The boy gazed at him, and not for the first time Bradford marveled at the almond perfection of Chinese skin, particularly around the eyes. At this kid's age he'd already had faint grey circles under his. From whacking off, his friends had said.

"Don't worry about it. If you can do that kind of work, you'll get in eventually."

They had a staring match, a contest which Bradford invariably won. The kid was going to have a hard life here.

Suddenly he was sick of all of them. The blacks and Latins who wouldn't play the game, the whites and Asians who often beat him at it. And the term hadn't even started yet. To calm himself, he resumed his number games, finishing one kid every 4.9 minutes. Outside it began to rain, and he opened his window so that he could hear the steady patter, feel the cool wet on the back of his neck.

9

At eleven-thirty his concentration was destroyed by the unmistakable bray of Rwanda Shabazz. He looked up and saw her in Gordon's cubicle, making some sort of emotive explanation, with gestures. She was absurd for many reasons, but today he was particularly appalled by her grating voice; by her do, a hundred small tufts of hair close against her scalp, a styling which revealed her elongated skull and suggested a botched high-forceps delivery; and by her earrings, immense gold hoops which he hoped to see her snag on something.

Still, though he despised her, he hoped she had come to work. If so, he could take a lunch break, go to Dullea's have a few belts. Chew breath mints afterward. With regard to Shabazz, however, hope of any sort was unwise; he bent his head and went back to work. Over-the-counter day was like the quarter-mile, which he had run in high school. If you went all-out, red-lined it, took the pain, it was over quickly.

"WHAT DOG? WHERE?"

Bradford looked up to see Shabazz charging through the doorway of his cubicle. She started around his desk, bent slightly from the waist; then stopped. Behind thick glasses her large eyes flared.

"Huh?" Bradford rose.

The small Filipina he was helping swiveled her head and looked up at him in terror, as if trapped between large carnivores. He put a hand on her shoulder.

"WHERE?"

Bradford gestured toward the kid. "Rwanda. Cool it!"

"Mickey . . . . " Gordon took one gingerly step into the cubicle, then moved aside to point at the figure behind him, a young brunette in the uniform of an Animal Control Officer.

10

"I called her," said Bradford. "When I got here this morning, there was a dead dog in a box in the hallway. It's in the janitor's closet."

"WHAT KIND OF DOG?"

"Rwanda. For Christ's sake!"

Gordon Wong pointed. "Firs' floor?"

"Yes."

Shabazz ran from the cubicle. Gordon and the brunette followed.

Bradford looked at his Filipina. A single tear made its way down each cheek.

"Don't worry. People get upset sometimes. It's okay."

But it was not. A minute later Rwanda Shabazz began screaming in the far-off janitor's closet. Kids squealed in sympathy or startlement. Bradford sat still for several seconds, but at last decided he had to go, After all, he had found the fucking thing.

By the time he arrived Shabazz had stopped screaming. She sat cross-legged on the floor, sobbing, between the cardboard box and a shiny waxing machine. Bradford understood that the only person he could punish for this was Gordon. He took the principal's arm, squeezed it.

"Gordon. She's freaking out the kids."

"Iss her dog!"

"What?"

"King!"

Bradford sighed. "I'm sorry. But a dog is not a human being, and she is a credentialed administrator, and she is freaking out the kids. Rwanda? You hear what I'm saying?"

Shabazz raised her head. Her glasses had steamed over, Slowly, and with difficulty, she got up, swayed drunkenly.

"WHO <u>DID</u> THIS?"

"Rwanda, I have no idea."

"I THINK YOU DO!"

"No, no, Rwanda!" said Gordon.

"THIS MAN HATES ME! YOU KNOW THAT!"

"No!"

Again Shabazz turned toward Bradford. Her fists were clenched, but instead of charging, she took a step back and once more began to sob.

Bradford realized that she was afraid of him. She believed that he had killed her stupid dog, and she was afraid of him. It was not enough that he had seen through her from the beginning. It was not enough that he had exposed her malingering, her carelessness, and her incompetence in a score of administrative meetings. It was not enough that in a sane, serious, and moral world innocent of affirmative action, he could provide enough evidence to justify the instant revocation of her administrative credential. It had taken a delusion to make her afraid of him.

He was furious.

TWO

For student helpers, over-the-counter day was traditionally a four-hour assignment, and though Molly and some others volunteered to stay, Bradford dismissed them all at one o'clock. Forty-three kids, latecomers, remained to be programmed, and he brought all of them into the Counseling Center; where some had to sit on the floor. The old radiators hissed and thunked. Windows steamed up, and the room smelled of wet clothes. Bradford's anger faded, and he began to admire the way he was handling the situation. When Gordon came by to say that he was taking Rwanda home, he appeared to be trembling; the woman herself was still sniveling; but Bradford, the aggrieved party, had gotten the show back on the road.

Yet before long he felt guilty. He had wished the woman ill, and it had come to her.

And by mid-afternoon, when the adrenalin rush of crisis has passed, he grew tired. He made mistakes, lost time. At three o'clock Gordon called to say that he would not be back. Shabazz had called Morrell, who had promised to stop by her house; he had also instructed Gordon to wait for him. After hanging up Bradford counted the kids and knew he could not finish until after six. He was angry once more. When he finished with his current customer, he got up and left his cubicle.

"It's raining hard," he told the next in line. "I have to take down the flag." On his way to the main door he took deep, deliberate breaths. His dedication to the day's work now felt like weakness.

Damned niggers.

No. Fats was a black man. Rwanda Shabazz, however, was definitely a nigger. And both of them had fucked him over, Morrell by rejecting his appeal and tying up Gordon, Shabazz by shirking, by making preposterous accusations.

To hell with it. He'd quit, now. Damned right. As he lowered the sopping flag, as rain spattered in his hair and on his face, the decision freed him, made him feel brave and reckless. He'd send the kids home, have them report to him on Monday, make the time to deal with them.

But when he had hung the flag to dry in the caféteria kitchen and returned to the Counseling Center, weary faces reproached him. Some of the little booger-noses had waited four or five hours. He couldn't leave.

Much to his surprise, this change of heart was rewarded. They wore out before he did. In the next two hours, one by one, twelve kids came to the door of his cubicle and begged to be allowed to see him the following week. He was through at five o'clock.

When he got to the lobby, it was raining harder than ever, and he decided to wait for a let-up. Now that the work was done, he was perfectly content to dawdle. In the late afternoons of his youth, after football practice, he had often waited in this same place, and for the same reason. The weather, at least, did not change much from year to year. Could be counted on.

And the dim lobby happened to be Bradford's favorite place at Alexander Hamilton. Along the walls on either side of the doors, athletic trophies in glass cases reflected dull crescents of gold or silver light. Above them, framed photos of past graduation classes hung in neatly spaced rows almost to the ceiling. Making the sides of a square, four more cases in the center of the lobby contained academic awards—plaques, certificates, scrolls of merit. In a curious way, this place was timeless. Its most recent momentoes, the JV basketball trophy and the class picture for 1995, would have been difficult to find, for in the dimness all past years seemed equidistant from the present.

Now Bradford made a nostalgic tour, a short walk he took only when completely alone, and gazed at his own name on four team and two individual trophies. One of these days he would haul out the janitors' big ladder, climb high, and see what he had looked like in his graduation class. He suspected that he would like what he saw. He also suspected that he had become a teacher, and then an administrator, because he had had such a good time in high school. A much better time, certainly, than he was having now.

Soon the rain was lighter. Its sound was that of hands crushing an endless strip of paper. He went out, locked the door, and trotted to the classic Buick he had inherited from his father. The rain exhilarated him.

But as he reached the car and dug for his keys, something caught his eye. He stepped back for a better look. The right front tire was flat. He looked at the rear. Also flat. He walked around the hood, into the street, and checked the other two. They were okay. Then he squatted by the front right and studied it. It did not appear to be cut, but the rubber cap to the valve was gone. He stood up, groaning, and checked the rear tire. Same story.

Rickey Bradford. Had to be.

Shabazz?

Paranoia. But the suspicion inflated, made his chest tight. The crazy fucking woman was entirely capable of it. He saw her squatting beside the tire, her butt a yard wide in that absurd kente cloth, jamming a pencil point into the valve.

"What's the matter?"

Molly Marcus had stopped her car beside his. She observed him cooly, as she had upon noting his trembling hands. Her pale, soft face was the youngest thing about her.

"Flat tires."

Molly frowned. "More than one?"

"Two."

"God. You need a ride?"

For a moment Bradford could not speak, utterly absorbed by the possibility of being with Molly in her dark, shiny car.

"I'm about ten minutes from here."

"I have time."

Walking around the trunk, he noted the Mercedes logo. As he opened the door, there was thrilling, portentous thunder.

"Nice wheels. Yours?"

"My father's."

"What are you doing around here now?"

"Some of us went to the gym to work out. Didn't you hear us?"

"No. How did you get in?"

"I have to take the Fifth on that."

"Okay. Go up Masonic, over the hill. I'll direct you from there."

They were silent until she stopped for the traffic light at Haight.

"Sorry about the smell. My father smokes a pipe."

"No problem."

More silence.

"Why would somebody do that?"

"The tires?"

"The dog."

"Oh. I don't have a clue."

She turned her head, gave him that small, wry smile. "You're lucky you still have a car, Mr. Bad Cop."

"Of course. How foolish of me."

"I'll bet Rickey Bradford did them."

"You know him, then."

"Slightly."

Bradford glanced sideways, saw that her raincoat covered the lovely thighs. He was just as glad. Talking to her was difficult even without the distraction, though the general experience was not really new. It repeated itself in the life of any male teacher who did not have two heads. The girls came along, new ones every year, and sooner or later there was chemistry, sometimes quite a lot. His first impression of them was always the same; they seemed grown, seventeen going on thirty. Still, he had never touched one, and usually the truth became inescapable: the girl was still a child in too many ways. So why was he messing with Molly? He couldn't seem to help himself.

"I can't imagine anybody hating her that much. She's just . . . ."

"What?"

"Sort of . . . scattered."

"That's one of way of putting it."

Another silence. Molly crested Masonic Avenue, and then Bradford directed her to Roosevelt Way, Levant, and States.

"You think it's racial?" Molly asked.

"I guess it could be."

"Some of the teachers really don't like her."

"You think a teacher did it?"

"God, I don't know. I know you didn't."

17

"You heard her."

"Everybody did."

"Just between the two of us, why do you think it might have been a teacher."

"You hear them talk about her. And the kids don't care enough."

"About race?"

"About adults. About what they do."

"My house is the gray one on the right."

"Hey. That's really nice!"

"Yeah. My father put in a lot of work."

"The whole neighborhood is, but this is really special."

Suddenly there was a heavy downpour. Bradford gazed through the windshield, into the sliding mass of silvery raindrops, and felt himself about to fall. As in downhill skiing, which he had once loved and been no good at. Going faster and faster, then knowing you've lost control and not, for the moment, caring at all.

He took her hand.

"Come on in. I'll show you the place."

"What?"

"I'll make us tea or coffee. There's a terrific view from the back."

He saw her take a deep breath, let it go.

"When you flirt with me, you're just teasing, right? Like I do with you?"

"No."

"You're not."

"No."

"God." Molly lifted her other hand from the wheel, a quick gesture of confusion. "What do I say now?"

"'I'd love to see your house.'"

"Oh, sure!" She seemed to look at his shoes. "I'm not ready for this."

"That's okay. I just had to be honest for once. I live neck-deep in bullshit."

"I know it's partly my fault. I—"

"—It certainly is not."

After a moment she said, "I'm gonna make a confession, all right? If you want to ruin my life, just tell people."

"Wow! I can't wait!"

"I'm a virgin, okay?"

"Of course it's okay."

"Very uncool."

"Have things really changed that much?"

"I'm just not sure I'm ready."

"I understand."

"Besides, I'm underage, you know. I won't be eighteen until—"

"—February fifteenth."

Silence.

"That's a little scary."

"I am not obsessed. If you get a heavy breather on the phone, it absolutely will not be me."

Silence.

"I have to go."

"Right." Bradford opened his door. "Thanks very much for the ride."

"You're welcome."

As he got out and shut the door, the window hummed, descended.

"Are you mad at me?"

"Of course not. Be careful driving home."

"Yes."

In the house Bradford peed, washed his hands, and then studied himself in the bathroom mirror, trying to decide whether Molly Marcus could possibly be interested in a man twice her age. He was reasonably encouraged. Despite the slight shading beneath his eyes, he had always looked

19

youthful and was rather vain about the fact. He had brown eyes. His features were regular, if soft and undramatic. Women sometimes called him attractive.

After putting on dry clothes, he poured himself a glass of Cabernet and stood before the big window in his father's den, looking at the view he had wanted to show Molly. Before him the mass of raindrops thinned and thickened in its steady, diagonal movement, and once more he thought of her, of the incredible legs and fanny, the brassy hair raining to her waist, the little-girl face and the grown-up irony. Suddenly there was a stretching, an aching, in his chest. The wind crooned, the raindrops murmured, the random splashes seemed to harmonize. He yearned for Molly Marcus, gave himself to the irresistible notion that if he could have her, not only her sex but her weight in his arms, her warm breath on his neck, her Chatelaine hair burning against his face, his life would change forever.

THREE

Bradford's favorite colleague, Janie Wetherall, referred to his office as The Thomas Gradgrind Memorial. Its chief furnishings were a monstrous blue-gray metal desk; an immense and quite official San Francisco City and County calendar, three square feet of marching black numerals; and an aged oak cupboard against a dull ochre wall. Above the door, too large for its short pole, was a brand-new American flag. For Bradford the general bareness was perversely satisfying, a tongue stuck out at his nest-building parents and others like them.

Among the papers on his desk Bradford located the final Advanced Placement essay of Jenifer Sharp.

Heroes of the People

The tone of the peom "Easter 1916" Is the idea that Yeats friends were great Heros of the irish revolution of 1916. The writer communicates his tone with good dicktion, Metaphors and ideas. In one long pargraph of the peom the poet gives his tone with words that are so positive in conotation. 'Sweet young and beautiful.' These words refer to one of the young ladies who was a member of the revolution. Other positive words like 'sensitive, daring, and sweet' are used about the mens . . . .

Bradford could read no further. He vaguely remembered liking the poem in college, and the girl's abuse of it made him indignant. He sat gazing at <u>Jenifer</u> and was soon reflecting on the stupidity, the cruelty, of sending a child through life with a deformed name. Of course for all he knew about black culture—or African-American culture, as Jesse Jackson now required—it might include the conscious fashion of using variant spellings of names popular with the white majority; for on the roster of Alexander Hamilton were a score of monikers like Jenifer, Yulanda, Phyliss, Markus, Leeza, and even Jone. But his guess was that the parents just couldn't fucking spell.

Joe Hensley walked in. Bradford saluted and spoke loudly. Hensley had one bad ear.

"Good afternoon, Colonel, <u>Sir</u>!"

"At ease."

Tall and broad-shouldered, Hensley was seventy-one years old, well past the usual retirement age. In the gray office light he seemed massive, hewn from stone. His voice was a thumping bass. In these and other ways he was a phenomenon, famous throughout the district.

"What's up?"

Hensley folded his arms, looked away. When he wanted to put people at ease, he kept his distance and averted his eyes.

"I gather you're about to referee a meeting."

"Yeah. Janie, Rohrer, and some parent."

22

"Can you get her out of it?"

"If necessary. Why?"

Hensley stepped to the window, looked out. "I know she spent the weekend in bed. She says she's all right now, but she looks peaked."

Bradford considered, his fingertips beating a brief rhythm on the desk. Once, with a bad migraine, Janie had fainted in her classroom. The event had been particularly disturbing to Hensley, who had been the first to reach her.

"I'll call her. If she wants, I'll certainly postpone it."

"She won't ask."

Bradford nodded.

Hensley turned, gave him a cross look. "Just cancel it. Tell them you're sick."

Bradford shook his head. "I'm not an essential party. Rohrer would just want to bring in Gordon. Or, God forbid, Rwanda."

The Colonel took two steps toward Bradford and was at last his stern and looming self. "Come on, Mick. You're the real boss around here. Just postpone it!"

"What's this all about?" Janie stood in the doorway, tall and pale, with fading freckles. "As if I didn't know."

"Joe was just saying you haven't been feeling well."

"I'm all right."

"Janie. I do not want to pick you up off the floor again. It is humiliating for both of us."

"Joe." She went to Hensley, poked his shirtfront lightly with a forefinger. "You are, as always, a dear. But buzz off."

When the Colonel had gone, Janie took the bad kids' chair, directly in front of Bradford's desk.

"Sometimes, around here, you'd never know it was 1995."

Bradford raised a hand, as if to fend her off. "Hey. I was standing for your rights."

"I should hope so."

They inspected one another. Janie had wide-set blue eyes and a shapely mouth. She was one of those people who look perpetually hopeful, or at least interested.

"We _can_ do this another day."

"No. I want to get it over with. Where are they?"

"I dunno. And I can't imagine what they think they have to complain about." Bradford held up Sharp's essay, then tossed it on the desk. "This is absolute, utter garbage."

"Oh. Not quite."

"If I were the kid's mother, I'd be ashamed to discuss it in public."

"Mickey." Janie sat perfectly straight. Like Joe Hensley, she was always at attention. "Don't patronize."

"I mean it!"

"I know what the paper is worth."

"Okay, okay."

"However—I am grateful for your support. I don't know quite what to expect from Rohrer."

"Uh-huh."

"Do you?"

"I think so."

"Good." Janie opened her purse, looked into it. "Before they get here, I want to show you something."

She found a newspaper clipping and handed it to him. Bradford read in the gray light. He had trouble concentrating. The article dealt with the Superintendent's remarks at a Board meeting. He had spoken of abolishing tracked classes and elite schools, of replacing them with programs of "collaborative learning."

"Same old, same old."

"He has a reputation to make, you know. He could be serious."

"Maybe. But his own people will tell him that it won't fly."

24

With her gaze she coaxed him toward the proper attitude. "We should have a meeting. Talk about it."

Bradford shrugged. On occasion, benighted egalitarians had tried to shut down Hamilton and been thwarted by its powerful alumni—whose power, to be sure, was waning. But Bradford felt the school was now rather like a monastery in a country under occupation. The triumphant barbarians had a certain superstitious respect for the faith of the vanquished, and so far they had left the place alone.

Just then two of the barbarians, Rohrer and the kid's mother, entered the outer office. The sight of the woman arrested Bradford. She was fat and ugly, like Rwanda Shabazz. Her tailored red suit made her resemble an overripe tomato. A vague discomfort came over him, then sharpened and became a distinct apprehension. The coincidence seemed ominous, as if the powers that be, worldly or unseen, were up to something.

Fuck it. He'd take no shit from this one either.

"Good afternoon." Rohrer stopped in the doorway, awaiting permission to enter. He was a counselor, the school's official Ombudsman for Minorities, and excessive politeness was one of his numbers. In his wire-rimmed glasses, baggy gray slacks, and rumpled blue blazer, he was like somebody out of French film, a shabby, pint-sized Noiret or Belmondo.

Bradford gestured toward two empty chairs. Sinking into one, Mrs. Sharp groaned, and Bradford set his jaw, locking up a grin.

"My understanding is that we're here to discuss two issues," he said after a moment. "The kid's grade and her dismissal from Honors?"

Rohrer looked at Sharp, she at him. Bradford's odd impression was that each felt he had revealed himself in some appalling way.

Rohrer nodded.

"I can't understand why she ended up with a C," said Mrs. Sharp. "Especially when she had a B at mid-term."

"Mid-term?" Bradford pretended confusion. "We don't give mid-term grades."

"I think Mrs. Sharp has reference to the second report period's grade." Janie gave Bradford a knowing look. Everything about her bespoke reason, order, restraint. She drove him crazy sometimes.

"I see. What was the grade for the first report?"

"A C." Janie looked at Rohrer. "By the way, the second report's grade was a B-, not a B."

Mrs. Sharp held out her hands, close together, as if understanding were an object that might be placed in them. "But she was getting better, wasn't she?"

"For a while. But she didn't sustain the improvement."

"If I may ask," began Rohrer. "Was the final paper a large factor in the determination of Jenifer's grade?"

"One factor," said Janie.

"Significant, then."

"Yes. Though two of her other essays in that final period were also weak."

"What were the grades on those?" Rohrer bowed his head, closed his eyes, as if to show himself possessed of monkish patience. His short hair lay close to his scalp, like *bas relief.*

Janie opened her grade book. Examining it, she blinked several times.

"A C- and a C. She also had two-B-'s."

"So. . . ." The lines of Rohrer's face sccmcd converge at the bridge of his nose. He opened his eyes and gazed straight ahead, as if Janie's words were printed before him.

The little fuck, thought Bradford. He thinks he's an actor.

"Would you say . . . those grades put her on the borderline?"

"Well--"

"--Look." Not for the first time Bradford sensed, at least faintly, that a serious discussion of capital letters—followed, or not, by plus or minus marks—was somehow ridiculous. But he plunged ahead, playing the innocent logician. "A C-, a C, and two B-'s average out to a C+, don't they? And with that last C-, they clearly warrant a C for the third report and a C final."

Now Rohrer examined him with—what? Contempt? Utter detachment? Profound moral sorrow? Rohrer had studied with Marcuse at UC San Diego. Am I a mere pawn in the historical struggle, wondered Bradford, or just a scoundrel?

Rohrer turned his head—a slow, onstage movement--and looked at Janie. "Is it as cut-and-dried as all that?"

"Not quite. A final grade isn't always an average. It does matter that Jenifer made some improvement during the semester. It does matter that she wrote two solid B papers in the second report. But this is Advanced Placement. It substitutes for English 1A at the University, and if I give Jenifer a B, I'm saying she doesn't need 1A. But the evidence is overwhelming—she does need it!"

"May we look at that final essay?" asked Rohrer.

"Certainly." Bradford picked it up the paper, tossed it to the edge of the desk, not about to pay Rohrer the courtesy of handing it to him.

Rohrer read the essay, gave it to Mrs. Sharp. "Certainly there are errors in spelling and mechanics. But you feel that the content is also unsatisfactory?"

"Yes. She misses a whole dimension of the tone—in fact, she ignores two entire stanzas "

"I'm not very literary," said Rohrer. "What is tone, exactly."

"Feeling and sometimes belief. In this poem it's mostly feeling."

"What I don't get is, why are the kids reading this kind of stuff anyway?" said Mrs. Sharp. "Who's this ol' poem about, anyway?"

"Participants in the Easter Rebellion of 1916," said Janie. "In Ireland."

"In Ireland? 1916? What's that got to do with the lives of these kids?"

"Whoa," said Bradford. "The relevance of the material is not at issue here. We're talking about the grade."

"But how can the child get a good grade if the stuff doesn't mean anything her?"

Janie sighed. "One of our tasks here is to impart—"

"--Wait a sec, Miss Wetherall." Bradford leaned forward, put his hands flat on the desk. "The material is in the text. The text has been adopted by the Board of Education. The relevance of the material is absolutely not an issue."

"Strictly speaking," said Rohrer. "But as a practical matter I hope we all recognize—I'll bet Miss Wetherall does anyway—that somebody like Jenifer is at a cultural disadvantage in dealing with literature of this sort. I wonder whether or not that disadvantage shouldn't be taken into consideration here."

"At this level," began Janie, "I think not. Next year, at the University, she will have to compete with other students on equal terms."

When Rohrer did not reply, she went on. "A moment ago you mentioned the mechanical errors. I agree that they shouldn't be the single determinant of the grade, but they affect content and result, in part, from her confusion about her subject. And she makes a huge number of them."

"Of course some are matters of dialect—hers as opposed to yours."

"'My dialect,' I think, is that of the University and professional world beyond it. Most AP students hope to do well in both."

Rohrer glanced aside, hesitated. At last he said, "Your arguments are clear and emphatic, Miss Wetherall. The upshot, I guess, is that you're not willing to change the grade."

"No. I am not."

Rohrer turned to Mrs. Sharp and spoke slowly, as if translating from a foreign language. "The Education Code says that the teacher has the sole right to determine a child's grade, unless there's evidence of incompetence or bad faith. We're not prepared, I think, to make an argument in regard to either of those. So perhaps we should pass on to the next issue."

Mrs. Sharp grimaced, then shrugged. *Incompetence* and *bad faith* brought color to Janie's face. Rohrer looked at Bradford.

"Which is that of the child's removal from the AP Program."

"A matter of policy," said Bradford. From the litter on his desk he retrieved the English Curriculum Handbook, which he had folded open to the appropriate page. "'To remain in the Honors or Advanced Placement Program, students must consistently do A or B work.' With the C in Miss Wetherall's course, Jenifer now has two C's and two B's in four semesters in the program."

"If that's the case, then the policy hasn't been strictly enforced in the past."

"The teacher always has some discretion. He can take into consideration circumstances such as illness or family emergencies, which can influence a student's performance in any given semester." Bradford raised his eyebrows slightly, tried to regain the look of innocence. "Were there such circumstances in Jenifer's case?"

"Mr. Bradford," began Janie, "since both Jenifer and Mrs. Sharp want Jenifer to continue in the program, and since Jenifer has had two previous B's in honors, I am

29

willing to withdraw my recommendation that she be dropped from the program."

"So it really is a matter of recommendation," said Rohrer.

In his lap Bradford clenched his fists. He looked at Janie, and she looked back, without blinking.

"You're sure."

"Yes."

"Very well. I defer to Miss Wetherall's judgment. You understand, Mrs. Sharp, that at this point, ten days into the term, I might have to make major changes in Jenifer's program in order to—"

—"No you won't," said Rohrer. "There's an AP in the same period as her present class."

Bradford gritted, then ungritted, his teeth. "Very well. Our business is concluded, then?"

No one answered. One by one they rose, Mrs. Sharp with difficulty. Looking at her, Bradford resisted pity. Why did they let themselves get like that? She ignored him, nodded to Janie, and then turned slowly, like a freighter coming about, and waddled toward the door. Following, Roher spoke over his shoulder.

"Miss Wetherall. Mr. Bradford. Thank you."

When they were gone, Janie and Bradford sat down again.

"You're angry."

Bradford made a face, bared his teeth. "Miss Wetherall! Have you no killer instinct?"

"So sorry."

"You had him on queer street! Finish him off!"

"I didn't think it was worth it."

Bradford clasped his hands behind his neck, stretched fiercely. He needed a workout, bad. "Your decision, of course. Anyway, the rest was nice. You really kicked his little Marxist butt."

"Must you see everything in terms of combat?"

"These days, I seem to. Though I gotta admit--I'm sort of glad Rohrer's around. He's the only person in school less popular than I am."

"You're not unpopular."

"Ha!"

For a long moment neither spoke. It was after five, and the school felt empty except for a janitor thunking garbage cans in some far-off stairwell. Bradford gazed at the mottled sky beyond the side window. It was very cold out; had been for days. A sadness pervaded.

He spoke slowly. "Do you ever suspect."

"Yes?"

"Do you ever suspect, despite all the splendid exceptions, despite all the propaganda, that they really are dumber than the rest of us?"

"Who?"

"Blacks. On average."

"Oh, God, Mickey!"

"Truth time. In the deep recesses of your intellect. In your heart of hearts."

She studied him before replying. "Some conjecture may be . . . simply too dangerous."

"Is that a denial?"

"If I hadn't been for that awful business with Rwanda, you wouldn't be saying this."

"Maybe not. But I'd be thinking it."

"Really?"

Bradford raised his hands, enumerated his points on the fingers of one. "Seventy percent born out of wedlock. Nearly a third on welfare. One standard deviation below whites on any I.Q. test you care to give 'em. Fifty percent of the young males, in California, on probation or in jail. And all this after thirty years of affirmative action and fifty billion dollars in anti-poverty money."

31

"It's too complicated, Mickey. Genetics, economics, psychology, sociology, history. One can't know."

"Okay. But I believe. On the basis of the facts cited, and on the basis of my own experience. Big Brother tells me one thing, I see another."

"Assuming you're right, what's to be done?"

"I'm not sure. Something."

"That's what worries me. The something." Janie stood up. "What I'm going to do is go home. And I certainly hope this office isn't bugged."

"Next year. B.B. has telescreens on order."

On his way out Bradford stopped in the men's, which smelled of shit. Rohrer was at the basin, washing his hands. Peeing, Bradford somehow felt there would be some loss of face in simply ignoring the little bastard.

"I trust your client is happy."

"I think she's exhausted."

"From battling the dastardly white establishment."

"It's no joke to her. Or me. She simply wants to keep the kid in a program she likes."

"And to mau-mau the teacher into changing the grade."

"She wanted an explanation of it. Which Miss Wetherall provided and she accepted."

People, thought Bradford, should move their fucking bowels at home. "She wasn't interested in the explanation. At the first opportunity she tried to divert the issue."

"The woman's not a collegiate debater, and the discussion was more than an exercise in logic-chopping—for the rest of us, anyway. It was about meeting the needs of a promising kid."

"Promising, my ass. To begin with, she got herself affirmative-actioned into the place. Since arriving, she has a 2.4 academic GPA and five final U's in citizenship. She's

32

taken the SAT's three fucking times and <u>still</u> can't break nine hundred."

"There's more to success in the world than test scores and meeting the expectations of school people. And you know it."

Bradford thought of hitting him. He'd bounce off the basin, the wall, the trash can, the floor. Like a pinball.

Instead Bradford took a breath, through his mouth, and then spoke. "Maybe we should just close up shop. Since our expectations are beside the point."

"I agree."

Bradford had been thinking of high school in general. It dawned on him that Rohrer meant something else.

"You support the Supe, huh?"

"Yes. And you people are just doing yourselves in. You won't give an inch."

"Because miles have been taken."

"Well. We'll see what happens."

"You bet."

FOUR

On the following afternoon, before a late meeting called suddenly by Fats Morrell, Bradford found himself with a half hour to kill, and so he went to the Tutoring Center. He had had a small part in its creation and felt obliged to work there. These days it was a pleasant refuge, a place quite unlike an office or classroom. Each month Gwen Chan put up a new set of reproductions from her collection of Impressionists. A donated CD player softly rendered serious music. Bradford had hunted through the district's warehouses for the round, walnut-colored tables. To provide nearly-matching captain's chairs, he had with questionable legality diverted certain funds from the maintenance budget.

The first person he saw was the tall Chinese sophomore to whom he had nearly assigned junior courses and to whom he had conveyed, no doubt bewilderingly, his momentary rage at students in general. He decided he would try to make amends. He took the chair opposite the kid, who had watched him cross the room. Despite their previous encounter the boy was again wide-eyed and hopeful-looking. After two weeks' growth his hair lay flat. He was Prince Valiant with a slightly ragged bang.

"Hi. What do you need help with?"

"Math. An' English."

"I'm not much of a math student. Let's see the English."

"I mus' write composition. Mus' be three hundred word. I only have one hundred-eighty-seven."

"Let's have a look."

As Beethoven's *Pastorale* played faintly in the background, the boy produced the paper from his binder, gave it to Bradford with both hands. Ceremonially, Bradford thought. He read it. Heart sinking.

"How long have you been in this country, Albert?"

"Two year."

"Uh-huh. Well, look—the paper isn't long enough because it's too general. You have to talk about particular things your parents and aunts do for you."

In the next fifteen minutes Bradford elicited, and noted in phrases, ten specifics. He slid the list across to Albert.

"Talk about these, and you'll have a paper that's long enough."

"Thank you. Can you help with grammar?"

Bradford sighed. In the short draft he could have marked thirty mistakes. He looked at the clock.

"I have to go in a few minutes. Let's concentrate on one thing."

Bradford wrote out the two major rules of subject-verb agreement and four exemplary sentences. He explained how the rules applied, and then they went over the paper. A third of the errors the boy now saw; the rest Bradford pointed out.

"We do es'ercises about this. I get them right, but when I write myself . . . ."

"I know. Look, we'll talk again, okay? I've gotta go now. You just have to keep at it."

"How come, if <u>you</u> is one person, I don' use <u>was</u>?"

Bradford did not know the answer. "English isn't always logical. Sometimes we do things just because they've always been done that way."

The boy looked disappointed.

"Learning a new language is difficult. You can't get it overnight."

Or over decade, thought Bradford, heading for the door. Maybe not over lifetime. The kid was eager and bright enough, but he might never <u>really</u> get it. Bradford was not sure that immigration was ever a very good idea; and, in the hallway, the sight of Gordon Wong approaching reinforced the doubt.

"Fats here yet?"

"Not Fats!" Gordon whispered. "Superintenden'!"

"No shit."

"Come on!"

In his office Gordon introduced Bradford to Superintendent Alomar, a short, stocky man with a thick nose, a Zapata mustache, and a trace of five o'clock shadow. Without the four-hundred dollar suit, he might have been a cut man in the corner of an East L.A. pug.

They sat down.

"We need to talk about Ms. Shabazz' troubles."

Gordon and Bradford nodded.

"First, let me say that she won't return to Hamilton. The situation is simply too . . . unpleasant. We'll try to have a replacement for you, Mr. Wong, by the end of next week."

Alomar shifted in his chair, clasped his hands in his lap, and looked at Bradford. "And to you, Sir, let me say that for Ms. Shabazz to have made the accusations she made, without evidence and in front of the children, was inexcusable. A letter to that effect will be placed in her file."

"As far as I'm concerned, that's not necessary."

"You're not . . . offended?"

"I am. But I can handle it on my own."

Alomar cocked his head slightly. "Really. How would you handle it on your own?"

Gazing at Alomar's heavy brown oxfords, Bradford concluded, with some disappointment, that they did not have lifts. "What I mean is, I can issue my own reproofs."

"I see." Alomar paused. "But you understand that I cannot countenance such accusations, anywhere in the district. As superintendent, I have to . . . take measures."

Bradford shrugged.

"That said, I'd like to know more about Ms. Shabazz' difficulties here. She seems to believe that from the beginning she encountered a great deal of hostility. I grant you that she is a very emotional woman and probably inclined to exaggerate. Still—I sat with her for nearly an hour and listened to a great outpouring of grievances. Often she wasn't very clear, but it's difficult to believe that she was making it all up."

"For example?"

"Ah. Well, Mr. Bradford, she complains that you were constantly critical of her in your administrative council meetings."

"That's not quite an example."

"She says that every time she makes a special schedule for a rally or assembly or whatever, you are critical. Specific enough?"

"Yes. The problem is, she makes them without consulting anybody and without looking at the school's calendar or the district's. In May of last year, for example, she scheduled a rally for the afternoon of the annual ROTC inspection. When informed of this fact, she moved the rally to the morning, where it interfered with the administration of three AP Exams. In the fall of last year, she scheduled the College Fair, the day when all the recruiters come, for one of the Jewish holidays. My phone didn't stop ringing for days. I could go on and on."

37

"Mr. Wong: will you confirm all this?"

"She make mistakes like that, yes."

"Constantly?"

Gordon squirmed. "Pretty of'en."

"Did you speak to her about them?"

"Yes."

"With what result?"

"She . . . remembers for a while. Then forgets."

"Her evaluations for last year, which you wrote, do not indicate a problem of such magnitude."

"I thought she would get better. Eventually."

Alomar bowed his head for a moment, seemed to consider. Then looked up.

"Mr. Bradford. Ms. Shabazz speaks of conflicts with the custodial staff. Which you supervise?"

"Yes. When she's upset, she treats them like shit. So—whenever possible, in ways I can't write them up for--they make life difficult for her."

"How? Tell me, please."

"They don't answer the summoning bells, claiming she's rung the wrong code. Which of course she does, sometimes. When she leaves her keys home, it turns out they've 'misplaced' whichever one she needs. Stuff like that."

"And what about the teachers?"

"Same story, essentially. Except that they're more subtle."

Alomar looked sideways, folded his arms. Then looked back at Bradford. "I have to point out that there's nothing about this sort of thing in any of her evaluations from other schools."

"How long has been been an AP?" asked Bradford.

"I believe this is her third year."

"So it's just two schools, this and Che Guevara."

38

"Yes. All right. I think so. I should double-check that. Still--why do you think she had no problems there?"

Bradford sighed. "Well. I have a theory. If you want to hear it."

"By all means."

Bradford gazed at him. He had decided that, personally, Alomar was perhaps not a bad sort. He was, however, an educational carpetbagger, one of a class which Bradford despised. Alomar had run three school districts in ten years, and rumor had it that he was headed for New York City. And in that moment, he was to Bradford rather like a big-time quarterback with great protection. You were lucky to get one good shot at him all game long, and you wanted to be sure that he remembered you.

"Che Guevara is a dumping ground. Hamilton is a school. Here people are trying to teach, or to make teaching possible, and when somebody like Rwanda screws up, they get pissed off."

Alomar gazed at him. "Including you."

"Yes."

"You don't think people at Guevara do the best the can?"

"Some do, I have no doubt . In a rather depressed state of mind. Others are just cashing their checks."

"You yourself have never taught in such a place."

"No."

"Yet you feel competent to judge."

"To an extent, yes. First-hand experience is not the only valid kind. I've talked to people who work there. I've seen the lousy test scores and the figures on suspensions and dropouts."

"Mr. Bradford, do you have any idea who killed Ms. Shabazz' dog?"

"I do not."

39

"Despite the fact that you know all these people who detest her."

"Very few people kill animals. Except for food."

"Yes. But you, Mr. Bradford, are in the eye of this particular hurricane. It seemed to me possible that you might know something."

"I do not. As I told the investigating officer."

"Did he tell you how serious the matter is, legally? That it was a felony, a hate crime?"

"He told me they were investigating it as such. He also said that until somebody was arrested and charged, it wasn't anything."

Alomar hesitated, then said, "You know, Mr. Bradford, it seems to me that you are as upset as Ms. Shabazz."

Bradford laughed. "No. I don't think so."

"Your self-control is impressive. Still, I feel it. Mr. Wong, do you?"

"What?"

Gordon did not appear to understand the question.

"I see. Well. No need in prolonging this." Alomar stood up. "Gentleman, I thank you for your time and your frankness. I feel bound to say, however, that I may make other changes here. For the good of all, I hope. The atmosphere seems . . . not good. But nothing will happen until I've spoken to Mr. Morrell and perhaps others."

When Alomar had gone Bradford said, "Hey, Gordon. Think we'll be happy at Che Guevara?"

"Not funny!"

But they both laughed, and in that moment Bradford liked Gordon better than he ever had.

"Don't let him move you without a fight. You've got a contract. You've got the administrators' union. You're a Chinese principal in a school with a plurality of Chinese kids."

"He can still transfer me."

40

"Yeah. But you can raise a huge public stink, and these guys do not like huge public stinks. Make sure the bastard understands he'll pay a price."

"I jus' wan' to stay, do a good job."

"That's not always an option. But you don't have to take it lying down."

"What about you?"

"I'm just Acting, so they can fire me as AP anytime they want. But I won't go to another school. As teacher, I have tenure and seniority. I'll just bump that asshole Boylston back into the sub pool."

"If I stay, I need you."

"No you don't."

"I do."

"Ain't nobody indispensable."

"You know, I knew something like this would happen."

"Why?"

"Superintenden' right. About atmosphere."

"Alomar doesn't know shit about this school."

"Something's wrong. I know."

At nine o'clock that night, with the Forty-niners on the Saints' nine-yard-line, Bradford's phone rang. He turned down the sound, picked up the receiver.

"Hello?"

"Mick, this is Fats."

"Why Mr. Morrell! What a surprise!"

"Bad news."

"Bad _timing_! Young's rolling out, looking. Throwing for the corner. Aw, shit. They picked him off."

Morrell was silent.

"Okay. Let's have it."

"The Superintendent would like you to move on to Washington."

"No fucking way. I'll go back to the classroom."

41

"Washington is not a bad place, and you are a valuable administrator."

"Nope. They'll have to carry me out."

"I want you to know I spoke against this."

"Thank you."

"Do you believe me?"

"Of course."

A half-hour later Morrell called back.

"I'm embarrassed to ask this, but I'm also a practical man with practical problems. If your teaching program included a couple of free periods, would you help break in your successor?"

"No. Keep me where I am or put me back into the classroom."

"All right. Talk to you later."

Bradford turned off the ball game. He was quite pleased with his bravado and for more than an hour wandered about the house, sipping beer and occasionally repeating aloud some of his remarks to Morrell. At ten-thirty he decided he was being silly. He drank one scotch and water and went to bed, but couldn't sleep. At one he got up, drank more scotch. The house was bitter cold, and he turned the heat back on. At three he was still awake and slightly smashed. At last he went into the kitchen, drank a glass of milk and ate a glazed donut.

By then he had of course realized that he really--really-- did not want to lose his job. He had been a good enough teacher, but he was a first-rate administrator and did not want to teach again. He was also a cocky son-of-a-bitch, always had been, and had never truly believed that something like this could happen to him. But in his contempt for Alomar's breed he had overplayed his hand. He was out, and there was nothing he could do about it.

Except fucking kill somebody. He thought of his father's .38, upstairs in a bureau drawer. In the absence of strong unions, the firearm was the *de rigueur* labor management tool of the nineties. Boss fucks you over, you pack heat to the office, splash his brains all over the wall.

Then take out Shabazz too, for good measure. Bradford's revenge fantasies rarely included women, but he had trouble viewing Shabazz as female. She seemed androgynous, a tar-faced, cuntless monster.

In the bad moments of his life—of which there had not been, in truth, very many—Bradford always imagined doing terrible violence to his tormentors. When these visions faded, he felt foolish. They always seemed, at last, merely play.

FIVE

For a time Bradford had the meager consolation of *schadenfreude*. The cafeteria shut down for a day because no one showed up at six in the morning to receive a truckload of foodstuffs. Teachers stormed Gordon's office when the new AP's forgot to sign up students to man the supply room. No one distributed supervision assignments, and therefore no adults showed up for a Friday night dance. Locked out, the kids improvised, boogeying in the schoolyard to music from car stereos until neighbors called police, who arrested three drunken seniors. The yearly CTBS testing had to be postponed because no one knew where Shabazz had stored the test booklets. Bradford might have guessed their location but did not try; for, though he passed on factual information to his successor and Rwanda's, he refused to advise or speculate.

But it was not long before he knew the certain truth of the platitude he had expressed to Gordon: *ain't nobody indispensable*. Eventually students got their meals and took their tests. Teachers got chalk, binder paper, gradebooks, and blotters. The transfer of Shabazz and the demotion of Bradford ceased to be the chief topics of conversation in

44

the faculty lounge and the cafeteria. People conceded that the new AP's, though inexperienced, were trying to do a good job. Bradford's friends planned a protest for the next Board of Ed meeting, and nearly all of the teachers signed a petition on his behalf, but no one was optimistic about restoring him to what that document called "his rightful place."

During his lunch period he prowled the school, looking for Molly. Just the sight of her, he thought, would cheer him up. She was not to be found; and several days passed before he thought to check the absentee bulletin and discover that she was home with the flu. His new classes were okay but tedious; he soon recalled all his reasons for preferring administration to teaching. The work of an English teacher was never done; he spent the weekdays in class, the weekend grading and making lesson plans.

Even more important was a truth he had long ago recognized but never admitted to others. In fact he had forgotten it and would no doubt forget it again. Regarding it, perfect honesty would have been difficult and probably in poor taste; so when people asked why he liked being an AP, he had always said, "It's an interesting job. You get to see things other people don't." Or, even more vaguely, "Well, despite the hassles, it's unique. I've never had a job remotely like it." These remarks were true enough, but they did not get to the heart of the matter. The truth was that Bradford enjoyed power, however paltry his share of it had sometimes seemed.

After his demotion he spent much more time at home, and the experience was sometimes strange. Once, arriving at three-thirty, he opened the door to the lemony smell of soap and stopped suddenly in the doorway. Déjà vu. It was as if his mother had finished her housework and was lying down upstairs. In fact, she had been dead for several years;

45

the cleaning woman, whom he rarely saw, had just left. Now and often in the weeks to come Bradford had the peculiar sense that the ghosts of his parents kept the place in order.

In the bedroom he had occupied nearly all his life he took off his schoolclothes, put on trunks and sneakers, descended to a corner of the garage, and, using his mother's old kitchen timer to measure out three-minute rounds, went toe-to-toe with the Everlast heavy bag.

Bradford loved boxing. Through junior high and in his first year of high school, he had trained and fought at the Columbia Park Boys Club. Three weeks after his sixteenth birthday he had begged the club coach to enter him as a novice light-heavy in the local Golden Gloves tournament. Ahead on points in the third round of his first bout, he had been knocked cold by a left hook he never saw, after which the coach refused to let him into the ring. "You gotta glass jaw, Big Guy. A real puncher might kill ya." Though ashamed, Bradford respected the man and took his advice; he was not interested in being killed. Still, he missed the ring and had never stopped working out on the heavy bag, which did not have a left hook or any other punch.

After his shower he rewarded himself with a double bourbon on the rocks while preparing a meal of bread, canned fruit, and a *Lean Cuisine* entrée. With dinner he drank half a bottle of a good Chablis or Cabernet, and when he collapsed into the black leather recliner in his father's den, he was too tired and dopey to do much except watch sports on the tube, though later in the evening he required himself to read for an hour before bed. For more than a month he had been moving slowly, ten pages at a time, up *The Magic Mountain*.

On occasion, however, he turned off ESPN, sat in the dark, and considered changing his life. It seemed a bit late, though, for a new profession. The most plausible and appealing possibility was to take a year off for travel. To finance this step, he would have to sell the house, and now was definitely the time. Admirable from without, the place grew seedy within. In the dark Bradford felt the cracking leather of the recliner beneath his fingertips, and its sharp, unpleasant texture was a synecdoche for all that was happening throughout the entire structure.

Six months earlier, Tom Halliday, his next-door neighbor, had offered Bradford both his services in selling the place and an estimate of its value—five hundred and fifty thousand dollars. To Bradford, this figure was simply one more benchmark, as if another were needed, of the looniness of modern times. Reason told him to take the money and run. But he had spent nearly his entire life in this house and something, perhaps no more than stubborness, made him want to keep it.

At the same time he often felt that he deserved neither it nor the proceeds from selling it; for, in his youth, his most serious troubles with his father had resulted from his unwillingness to learn any of the crafts with which he might now preserve and maintain it. While friends vexed their parents by drinking, messing up in school or totalling cars, Bradford's principal rebellion had been to disappear from home whenever he was scheduled to learn wiring, carpentry, painting, plastering, roofing, or plumbing, skills which his father, a building inspector for the city, considered necessary for any man. Bradford the boy had wanted only to box, play ball, or, when the rare opportunity presented itself, explore mysteries beneath the under-clothing of young females. When none of these activities was possible, he read in the public library, where his father never thought to look for him.

The conflict had not been greatly consequential.. Bradford's father had not been a harsh man, and in most ways Bradford had been a good boy. He kept his room clean, did his routine chores, and concealed his constant masturbation. He did well in school; some teachers thought him an ideal lad. His peccadillos were sexual, and he had had the good fortune to be caught in none of them.

And, his adolescent stubborness aside, no one could blame him for believing that finally he had done right by his parents; for he had nursed both, one after the other, through their last illnesses. In retrospect these duties did not seem like much trouble, though certainly he had been unhappy at the time. When his mother said to him, repeatedly if perhaps not quite sincerely, that she ought to go to a hospice and free him of the burden, he had always responded, "What else do I have to do?"

Indeed. The afflictions of his parents—cancer, in each case—had given him something to do with life after his divorce. In his early twenties Bradford had married a pretty, restless, and sexy woman he had met in teacher training. After earning their credentials both had taught in San Francisco, but Bradford's wife had burned out quickly and enrolled in the MBA program at Berkeley. Not long after taking her degree, she announced that "their lives were taking different directions" and proposed a trial separation. From her point of view this trial was a complete success, and the divorce became final three weeks before Bradford's thirtieth birthday. For a time Bradford felt bereft, unmanned; but before long he began seeing other women and soon brooded less about past abandonment than about possible future entrapment.

The marriage had been but one phase of a life which, now that he thought about it, divided itself neatly into phases. From the fifth grade on he had been an obsessive jock. After his brief boxing career he was a three-sport, three-year letterman at Hamilton. His coaches described him as a team leader but also hinted that he wasn't good enough to compete in college; and when he arrived at

Berkeley, he quickly discovered that they were correct. Despite this disappointment, his jock phase did not end. He became an intermural athlete and was at one time director of the intermural program. After college had come his marriage phase, followed by his nursing-mom-and-dad phase, and at last his adult-team-leader phase, in which he functioned as Acting Assistant Principal at Alexander Hamilton High School.

Bradford had become a school administrator almost by default. Like most young teachers, he took courses in the evening and summers, partly to earn the additional units necessary for placement in the district's highest salary classification; but he had been an especially persevering student in imitation of his ambitious wife. At first she herself studied school administration while Bradford began work on an M.A. in English. In Intro. to Grad. Study, however, he had difficulty mastering the conventions of the MLA Style Sheet; his academic advisor thought he really wasn't trying. The following semester, in Twentieth Century American Writers, he had a problem common to many contemporary graduate students: in his essays he found himself arguing propositions far more interesting to his professor, an early deconstructionist, than to himself.

When his wife switched from administration to business, Bradford was ready to give up school and stay home nights. But she argued that their trips to and from the campus, the meals in the cafeteria, provided them with Quality Time Together that should not be sacrificed. Moreover, Bradford sensed that she would not long endure a husband without ambition. Therefore he enrolled in the education courses she had taken the year before. One advantage of this move was that he did not have to buy texts; he could use hers.

As an academic subject, school administration proved just slightly more interesting than deconstructionism. Bradford studied for two years but abandoned his courses when his wife abandoned him. Then came some peculiar but consequential circumstances. High, unseen powers—Bradford was never sure whether they dwelt in the University, the State Legislature, or the State Department of Education—decided to change radically the requirements for the Administrative Credential in Secondary Education, invalidating some of the courses Bradford had taken and mandating one more full year of course work. But lower unseen powers—the teachers' unions, perhaps, or students who threatened litigation—wrung a concession from the greater: those laboring in the current program were to be grandfathered in, provided that they could pass an examination. Though Bradford's last education course was two years behind him when this dispensation was announced, he was still the inveterate competitor and decided to give the exam a shot. After a month of cramming, he passed by five points,

By that time he as already spending half of each work day supervising halls and handling cut clips; and when Jack Farnsworth had a mild coronary and took early retirement, Bradford was appointed Acting Assistant Principal for Curriculum and Maintenance. After five years on the job he was still Acting because he was the wrong color. It would be five or ten years before he got a real contract, and he was quite sure that he kept his place at Hamilton, a coveted assignment, only because every school needed at least one entirely competent administrator.

On a Friday several weeks after Bradford's return to teaching, Joe Hensley approached him in the hallway.

"I have some scuttlebutt which may be of interest to you. Care to stop by Dullea's on your way home?"

"I was gonna do that anyway."

"See you there."

In fact, Bradford had been planning to tie one on. He had not been truly drunk since summer, and he felt entitled, in view of his recent travail. Though a hangover would slow his paper-grading, he would have time for recovery— Monday was a holiday to celebrate "Indigenous People," who were replacing the politically incorrect Columbus. And now, as he watched the Colonel move away, Bradford found himself impatient at the thought of enduring a tete-a-tete before commencing his toot. But Joe had lately shown him unusual sympathy. He had called friends among the influential alumni and asked them to take up Bradford's cause. He had urged Bradford to file a grievance with the administrator's union and to consult a lawyer about the possibilities of suing Shabazz and/or the school district. Bradford had acted upon neither suggestion and was not eager to admit these omissions to his old teacher. He would feel exactly as he once had upon arriving at the Colonel's class without having done his homework.

After school he drove home, put his car away, and walked to Dullea's, a big, low-ceilinged joint with pool tables and a vintage Wurlitzer that played nothing recorded after 1965. The place had once catered chiefly to the Irish but now had a larger clientele which Bradford thought of as The Last of the White Guys.

For Bradford, Dullea's was evocative. Twenty years earlier it had been the informal clubhouse of the Cole Valley Boys, a civic group which had sponsored the Sunday ball team he had played for in his early teens. Once every few months, as player-manager, he had gone there to pick up new balls or bats and could remember escaping its pleasantly lurid confines—from his parents he had imbibed the notion that bars were places of pathology, even wickedness—to stand in the healthy sunshine and open a box of twelve glossy, white, red-stitched National League baseballs, even putting one against his tongue to taste its new leather.

Overhead at Dullea's one always heard skipping or shuffling feet or the slappety rhythm of the light bag, for upstairs was Billy Barton's gym, of which Kevin Dullea was landlord and part-owner. Minors were not allowed in Barton's, and when Joey Giardello had come to town, young Bradford had stood in the cold across the street, peering through the dusty windows to catch glimpses of the ex-champ or his shadow.

At sixteen, his face unpleasantly heated by three-days' growth of beard, Bradford had had his first illegal drink at Dullea's; five years later, to celebrate his defloration of a law student named Betty Schwarzbart, his first legal one. On the greasy walls were pennants, banners, memorabilia of the '46 Seals and the '62 Giants, photographs of local sports stars such as Leo Nomellini, Frankie Albert, and Hugh McElhenny; Grant Butcher, Pat Valentino, and Bobo Olson; Lefty O'Doul, Roy Nicely, and Dario Lodigiani; Hank Luisetti, Tony Psaltis, and Frank "Apples" Kudelka. Waiting at the bar for Hensley, Bradford found that he could identify each fading, sepia image by pose and outline.

"Hey, Mick."

"Hey, Jimmy." Jim Dullea, the bartender, was Kevin's youngest son. Bradford ordered bourbon-on-the-rocks.

"Guy in here lookin' for you last week," said Jimmy, setting down the drink.

"No kidding."

"Name's Harley somethin'?"

"Doesn't ring any bells."

"Said he used to play ball against you."

Bradford shrugged.

"I got your number somewhere. You want me to give it to him?"

Bradford shook his head. "I know too many people as it is."

Jimmy laughed, went away.

Hensley arrived with Wynn Wilson, a young janitor at Hamilton, one of Joe and Janie's proteges. They helped him with his night-school studies and refereed his quarrels with others on the staff. Bradford did not like the kid.

When their drinks came, Hensley put a big hand on Wilson's shoulder. "Wynn, I need a private word with Mick. We shall rejoin you shortly."

Wilson nodded, looking at his glass. He had not spoken.

On the way to a back table, Bradford said, "Now he's jealous."

"Really? Why?"

"He admires you and detests me."

"Why would he detest you?"

"I'm not sure."

"He has some rough older brothers, back in Texas. Perhaps he identifies you with them."

"Too bad."

They sat down. Spine straight, Joe rested his hands on his thighs. He had a familiar troubled look, as if worried that the ensuing conversation might somehow subvert his dignity.

"Very well. This is none of my business, of course. But I have some scuttlebutt from the Central Office about your removal. If you're interested."

"Hey. I love gossip."

"My source is one of the last of the old guard, a reliable fatherly sort. Alomar doesn't talk to him, but Alomar's boys do."

"Uh-huh."

"To me, it's all rather strange. Had you met the man before he came out to school?"

"Never."

"Apparently you really set him off."

"He has some rough older brothers, back in Tijuana."

The Colonel laughed thunderously. Men turned to look. "In his usual tremulous way, Gordon told us that you stood up to the man. But apparently there are a couple of other things. First that you protested the reinstatement of some black students. True?"

"Largely. One was white, though."

"Second, that some one at school—someone besides Shabazz—has denounced you as a racist."

Bradford nodded.

"Who, do you suppose?"

"Maybe Terry Lucas. Maybe John Rohrer."

"FUCK YOU, YOU BABOON!"

The Colonel and Bradford looked around. The pool players had straightened up One had shouted at the TV.

"FUCKIN' THIEF!" called another.

"Freddy Lamar," said Joe, gazing at the screen. "When I came back from Korea, there he was. There he has been. I fear he will outlast me."

"Could be."

In 1954 Freddy Lamar, a lank and laconic black man, had been elected to the Assembly from Bradford's district. He had been thrown out in 1960; re-elected in 1966; rejected once again in 1974; and re-elected in 1980. In the fourteen years since he had kept the office—chiefly, Bradford thought, through the inertia of his constituency. He was now a candidate for Mayor.

"Where were we?" said the Colonel. "Oh yes: Terry Lucas. His preposterous opinions notwithstanding, I don't believe he's vicious."

"More likely Rohrer."

"I would say so. Anyway, finally and most important. Alomar wants you out of Hamilton, and he has launched a quiet investigation. Someone is studying your file, and they are interviewing people about you."

"Who?"

"The only name my source had was one I've heard but can't place. Martha Collins?"

"Woman on the PTA Board. Liberal and passive-aggressive."

"I see. Well--that's about it. I trust I haven't spoiled your weekend."

"Thanks. I really don't think there's anything else they can do to me."

"Have you talked to a lawyer?"

Bradford looked away, shook his head.

"You should."

"I'm still thinking about it."

In the Colonel's look Bradford saw, or thought he saw, the question he had seen there twenty years ago: Will this boy amount to anything?

They went back to the bar. Bradford took the stool beside Wilson, partly to show he was willing to make an effort with the kid, partly to show he wasn't afraid of him. Ordering his second drink, he asked himself why such a gesture was necessary. Had no answer.

Again Joe put his hand on Wilson's shoulder. "Wynn just got his A.A., going at night."

"Hey." Bradford reached across his body, put out his hand. "Congratulations."

"Thank you." The kid shook hands but didn't look at Bradford. Wilson was a wiry, freckled red-head of medium height. His blue eyes were as bright and sharp as Hensley's were pale and indistinct.

"He's also applying to the Police Academy."

Wilson stared at his drink. Suddenly he straightened up, slid off his stool.

"'scuse me, Gents Gotta pee."

When he had gone, Bradford said, "See what I mean?"

"Say--I think I know what it is. Something he said to me not long ago. He thinks you have designs on our Miss Janie."

"Terrific."

Hensley laughed. "I didn't take it seriously at the time. I shall hasten to assure him that you have no chance with her."

"Good. In the meantime I'll watch my back."

When Wilson returned, he said, "Colonel, if I buy you a drink, will you tell us about the war?"

Hensley sipped his scotch and did not reply for several moments, gazing into the mirror behind the bar. "I don't believe I'm quite drunk enough."

"You said you would sometime."

Bradford saw a chance to please them both. "Hey, Joe. I'd like to hear that too."

Again the Colonel hesitated. "Also, I'm not sure you guys are old enough to listen with the proper attitude. War is not romance."

"I know that," said Wilson.

"Do you," said Hensley. In the mirror he looked morose. "And you, Mr. Bradford. Do you know that war is not romance?"

"Yes, Sir."

"I sense that you two have things in common. Perhaps some of the same illusions."

"Then disabuse us," said Bradford. "Give us the reality."

Still Hensley gazed into the mirror.

"Come on, Colonel!"

"The war came. I enlisted, patriot that I was. Physically I was precisely what they wanted. Twenty-ten eyesight. Excellent reflexes. I was trained and sent to fight, which I did. Passably."

"More than passably," said Bradford.

"That's what I hear too," said Wilson.

"He was an ace."

"Who told you that?"

"Jack Farnsworth."

The Colonel's face tightened. The line of his mouth stretched, the creases deepened.

"Technically, I was. Not actually."

"Explain, please," said Bradford.

"I had only three legitimate kills. The rest, I am mildly embarrassed to say, came in The Great Marianas Turkey Shoot."

"What was that?" asked Wilson.

"A naval air battle," said Bradford, eager to be the good student. "Late in the war."

"A slaughter, late in the war. They had already lost, but they sent up boys in junk planes." Joe looked first at Wilson, then Bradford. "Boys who thought war was romance. In thirty-five minutes I dispatched four of them to 'their Honorable Ancestors,' as we used to say in those days. I saw one of them burning to death in his cockpit."

"And they made you a Colonel," said Wilson.

"For Christ's sake, no! That came between the wars. When I was a desk jockey!"

"Still, you _did_ it," said Bradford. "Went to war and fought. Vanquished the enemy."

The Colonel turned his huge body and reached past Wilson to point at Bradford. "You listen here. You want to know what it was like. I shall tell you. And then the first one of you to mention it again gets a poke in the nose."

"Yes, Sir!"

"In those days people were still in awe of flight. It was dominance over nature, man become God. But the illusion did not survive one's first solo, much less combat. Blinding sun, blinding fog or clouds. Making mistake after mistake, despite your training. Overshooting, stalling out, banking so quickly the machine shook like a baby's rattle. Taking rounds from an enemy you could not see."

He paused. Wilson and Bradford nodded in reverence, almost in unison.

"Only one thing mattered, Young Gentlemen. Having the guts to do what you had to do. The problem is, you don't remember that part of it. You do not recall the moments of commitment for which you might justly congratulate yourself. All you remember is fear, danger, and confusion. So you see there is no nostalgia, no romance."

Silence. Then Wilson said, "Thank you, Colonel."

"Yes. Thanks."

"If on the morrow I decide that I have made a fool of myself, I shall find the means to make both of you pay."

They laughed.

Dullea's was filling up. There was talk and laughter, the click and thock of cues and balls, the clink of glasses and plates. It became difficult to hear, and the men from Hamilton talked less and drank more. For some reason Bradford found himself reconsidering a suspicion that had been in and out of mind for weeks, the idea that Wynn Wilson might have killed Shabazz' dog. At school there had been all sorts of conjecture as to the culprit; but as far as Bradford knew, the kid's name had never come up. But he had had access to Shabazz' address; the stealth and agility to hop her fence on Shrader Street; keys to the Hamilton plant; and a hatred for the woman beside which Bradford's distaste seemed positively mild. When Bradford had explained to Alomar why the janitors' disliked Shabazz, it was Wilson's fury which had been clearest in his memory.

Freddy Lamar reappeared on the six o'clock news, evoking more curses from the pool players. When he was followed by O.J. Simpson and his lawyers, they howled. And from another corner of the bar, a chant began, softly.

"Freddy Simpson, O.J. Lamar. Freddy Simpson, O.J. Lamar, Freddy Simpson, O.J.Lamar."

The pool players chimed in. "FREDDY SIMPSON, O.J. LAMAR!"

Bradford laughed. "What the fuck?"

Wilson pointed to a corner of the bar mirror, where someone—with scotch tape, newspaper headlines, and an old campaign bumper stick—had put together the words which now filled the room.

The Colonel stood up. "Come on, you guys."

As Bradford and Wilson followed him out, the place was in an uproar. Half the men shouted, most of the rest were laughing.

"FREDDY SIMPSON! O.J. LAMAR!"

When they reached the sidewalk, the chant ended with a cheer.

"Are we offended?" asked Bradford.

"We are politic," said the Colonel. "With all your other troubles, you don't need to be associated with that."

"Huh?"

"Milt Bolling was in there. With some other twerp whose name I can't recall."

"O'Neill," said Wilson.

"Oh yes. Simon O'Neill."

"The Balboa guys?" asked Bradford, mystified.

"No, No," said the Colonel. "They're both at Central Office now."

"Race traitors," said Wilson.

The Colonel laughed. Then he said, "Bolling has the Superintendent's ear."

"Which has what to do with me?"

The Colonel looked at him. "Don't be obtuse."

"You mean he might tell the Supe I was here? He'd be incriminating himself."

"He has an excuse. He's Jack Dullea's brother-in-law."

Bradford shook his head. "Colonel Machiavelli."

"The superintendent is Machiavelli."

They were quiet a moment, and then Wilson pointed to lighted windows above. "Hey. Let's go watch the guys work out."

Bradford and the Colonel looked up.

"I wouldn't mind clearing the cobwebs," said Hensley. "Before I get behind the wheel."

They went around the corner to the entrance, climbed its narrow stairway. A ceiling bulb was out, and the passage was darker than the street.

In the grimy fluorescence of the gym two black welterweights sparred listlessly. Billy Barton sat on a bench against the worn grainy wainscoting. He turned his head, squinted at the newcomers.

Bradford called out to him. "Okay if we watch a while, Mr. Barton?"

The old man nodded and resumed his study of the black kids.

"You know him?" asked Wilson.

Bradford shook his head. "Only by sight. When I was a kid, they wouldn't let us in here."

"In his youth, Mick was himself a fighter."

"No shit," said Wilson.

"Stick and move, Jimmy," called Barton.

"I was a kid who liked to box. Not a fighter."

"Where'd you do it?"

"Boys Club tournaments. The Golden Gloves once."

"How'd you do?"

"Okay at the Boys Club. In the Golden Gloves, I got my ass whipped."

"Oh yeah?" said Wilson. He seemed pleased.

"Thoroughly."

"Knocked out?" asked the Colonel.

"Knocked cold," said Bradford.

"Getcher chin down, for Chrissake," growled Barton.

One of the black kids backed away, looking at the old man. Then he raised a glove to his opponent and headed for his corner. The message was *No mas*, in the famous manner of Roberto Duran.

Billy Barton watched the boys dress and leave. Then he looked toward the men from Hamilton. "These kids can't take instruction. You hurt their feelings."

"We know all about that," said Bradford. "We work in schools."

Everybody laughed. Bradford was happy to please Billy Barton.

"Hey, Mister Bradford. Let's you an' me go a few rounds."

Bradford rolled his eyes. "Oh, man."

"Come on! I been fightin' all my life, but I never fought a real boxer!"

"I'm not a real boxer."

For the first time that evening their gazes met. Bradford saw the challenge, the contempt. Then he turned to the Colonel, gave him a see-what-I-mean look.

"Wynn," said the Colonel. "You are asking for trouble."

"I need a workout," said Wilson. He tapped Bradford's mid-section. "So does he."

"Young fella, you are outweighed and outclassed."

Wilson looked at Bradford. The blue eyes were like jewels. "I'll take my chances."

Bradford looked back. "Ask Mr. Barton."

"Cost fifteen bucks," said Barton, rather quickly. He probably needed the business. "An' ya gotta sign waivers."

Bradford felt heat in his face. He had been angry for three weeks and, despite his hours of pacing and cursing at home, had said scarcely a harsh word to anyone. He decided that Wilson would pay for all of it. He reached for his wallet.

"Hey! On me!" Grinning, Wilson handed Barton a twenty.

The old man brought the gloves and the waivers. Wilson stripped to the waist. Giggling, he struck the pose of an old-time fighter, hands too high, elbows away from his body. Bradford removed his jacket, rolled up his sleeves. His tie was already loose, and he decided there was no reason to take it off.

The Colonel folded his arms. "All right then. Perhaps this will be therapeutic."

Lacing on the gloves took a while, and by the time he was in the ring, Bradford had cooled off a bit. But he wanted to show off for the Colonel and Billy. He'd just jab Wilson silly, till he got tired of being hit.

Barton rang the bell.

For more than a minute neither landed a blow. Bradford stepped away from the kid's roundhouse swings, and his own jabs hit only leather. His timing was way off. Punching the heavy bag, he had conveniently forgotten, was nothing like fighting a man. Before long, though, he began to get the range. A jab caught the kid on the forehead, snapped his head back. Recovering, he charged. Bradford tied him up. After a bit more mutual futility Bradford landed a jab to the mouth. There was blood, instantly. Again Wilson charged, and Bradford clinched.

Then Wilson hit him on the break, A hard right to the jaw.

"Hey, hey!" cried Barton. "None a that!"

Bradford could not move. A numbness began in his neck, spread into his shoulder and down his arm.

Glass jaw.

Wilson rushed in. Bradford caught him, rolled him into the ropes, held on. The numbness went to one leg. If he let go of the kid, he would go down.

"Leggo, Man! Leggo."

Bradford could hold on no longer. Bracing himself against the rope, he pushed the kid away, hard. Wilson staggered backward.

Barton stepped in front of him, shook a finger under his nose. "No hittin' on the break!"

In the last moments of the clinch the numbness had begun to fade. Wilson had not hit him quite hard enough. Barton's intervention gave him several more seconds, and when Wilson charged, Bradford nailed him flush on the nose with the jab. The crack of bone was audible. Wilson fell straight back. His head and torso bounced off the canvas. He lay still a moment, and a beard of blood covered the lower half of his face.

After a moment the kid rolled onto his stomach, climbed to his feet, and began a staggering charge. Barton stepped in, cupped his hand at base of the kid's skull and pressed a towel to his face. Suddenly the Colonel was there too, holding Wilson's arm.

"Leggo! Leggo! I'm awwright!"

"Awwright? Shit!" Billy Barton laughed, then looked over his shoulder at Bradford. "Pretty good left."

Bradford climbed out of the ring. He was ecstatic. Years ago in some film he'd seen a fighter bounce off the canvas like that. Then he remembered. Ingemar Johansen, when Patterson knocked him out in the second fight.

He watched Barton and Hensley ease the kid through the ropes, sit him down on the bench. Billy kept the towel to his face, trying to stop the flow. All the blood might have worried Bradford, but the kid was making too much noise to be seriously hurt. Hensley bent close to him, spoke urgently in words Bradford could not quite hear.

At last the Colonel stood up, looked for Bradford, found him.

"Mickey, <u>Go home</u>. I'll run him down to emergency."

Bradford's mind went blank. He'd been expecting something else. Didn't know what.

"Go!"

Bradford picked up his jacket and headed for the door.

People, he thought, keep trying to get rid of me.

SIX

The next day Bradford rose late. He had a mild hangover, a bruised cheekbone, and a stiff back. After his shower and shave, he shadow-boxed, groaning, as if Wilson might be lurking downstairs. In the kitchen he stretched a bit, made toast and coffee, and sat down to read the paper. He was astonished to learn that in the polls Freddy Lamar trailed the incumbent by only four points.

As he finished his second cup of coffee, the <u>slip-slap</u> of mail coming through the slot made him start.

Among bills and junk was a legal-sized envelope with an address typed in ink that looked like soot. For some reason Bradford suspected a chain letter. With their lunatic promises of wealth, their vague threats of harm for breaking the chain, they were spooky.

Inside were two papers, one a note in the sooty ink.

"Dear Mr. B.—
Heard about your troubles.
Thought you might be interested in this.
A Friend

This was a flyer, printed on heavy bond paper with clean and glossy modern type.

TO ANOTHER <u>ONE</u>

Our communique must be anonymous, and you're probably suspicious. But read on.

You are a white native-born American, You know that "people of color" do not wish you well. But maybe you haven't realized the whole truth. After all, most of us are preoccupied with earning a living and taking care of our families.

The mud people are out to destroy you. They want your jobs. They want your property. They want your women. We believe it is time to fight. <u>Now</u>.

Because the government is dominated by mud people and brainwashed whites, we must fight a guerilla war, low-down and dirty. Our means are the anonymous call and the threatening letter, the ski mask and bandana, the fist and the boot. Ultimately the gun and the bomb.

We of <u>Ones and Twos</u> have other weapons. Weapons that the enemy, known to some of our comrades as the Zionist Occupation Army, can't overcome. They are singleness, anonymity, obscurity.

We don't have membership cards or membership rosters. Also we don't have newsletters or scheduled meetings. The reason is this: the most effective guerrila operations are the ones planned and carried out by a single individual. Or by two such individuals who know and trust each other completely.

We want you to join us. We want you to choose the one person who makes you maddest. The college dean who hands out scholarships to minority morons. The greaseball, gook, or jigaboo dummy who's been affirmative actioned into a good job, does bad work or none at all, and makes life miserable for every white in the workplace.

Call him anonymously from a public phone. Be quick so the call can't be traced. Tell him you'll cut his balls off and mail them to his wife, postpaid.

Or, get a lead pipe, put on a ski mask, catch the enemy alone, and smash his face.

And before you hang up, or when you let him have it, tell the enemy that you are a soldier in the ranks of <u>Ones and Twos</u>. Let him know we're out here, and tell him we'll be coming for his friends, too.

All this probably sounds pretty rough to you. But <u>look</u>—look at your own experience! Look at what the mud people have done to you, to all white Americans, in the last thirty years! When you've confronted the facts, we think you'll be ready to join us.

Think it over. And then <u>act</u>!

"Whoop-de-doo!" said Bradford. He began opening the bills.

But the broadside did not go into the garbage with the junk mail and torn envelopes. Eventually he tossed it into a drawer where he kept bills come due, remembering another recent item of unsolicited mail, a "book club" advertisement. This had featured a color photograph of a large man coupling with a girl or ten or eleven. Bradford had felt brief excitement and complicity, which had made him ashamed. Today the sequela was an uneasiness which, on top of his other difficulties, he did not need.

During a shopping trip to Laurel Village he wondered about the sender; and the only person he could think of, disturbingly, was Wynn Wilson. In all likelihood, however, it was someone he didn't know—someone who had read one of the very brief newspaper articles about Shabazz' dog, her transfer, and his demotion. Someone he did not know was thinking about him. Trying to further complicate his life.

Driving home, he was suddenly angry. Pathetic assholes. Deluded nincompoops, who didn't understand that nothing could be done. The enemy was too strong.

Of course he would be happy to see something done. He wanted revenge.

Home again, he called Joe Hensley.

"You rude lads will replace my bloody shirt," said the Colonel. "Or there will be two more trips to Mr. Barton's establishment."

"Yes. Absolutely. He okay?"

"His nose is broken. By the time I got him home, it was quite swollen."

"He really asked for it."

"Yes. The boy is a puzzle. I lectured him thoroughly about your essential good will. I'm not sure I got through."

"I'm not sure about my essential good will."

"I'll talk to Janie on Monday. She may have more influence than I."

"Frankly, I never understood what you guys see in the kid."

The Colonel sighed. "Before his elders, he's . . . quite humble. And earnest. You don't see that?"

"No. And I want to run something by you. Wilson hated Shabazz, and he has keys to the school. You think he might have killed the dog?"

"It never occurred to me. Maybe it should have. Is there any evidence you know of?"

"Purely circumstantial."

The Colonel paused. "Would you be comfortable notifying the authorities?"

"I guess not."

"Then don't."

Bradford was sometimes given to labyrinthine imaginings, and that night Wilson was their subject. In his bones and synapses, he still felt the ferocity of the kid's attack. It seemed inexplicable. Early on, the guy had seemed to like him. In fact, now that he thought about it, perhaps there had been something on the order of respect, or at least the earnestness that Janie and the Colonel apparently felt. But Wilson had begun having trouble with teachers and other janitors; and eventually Bradford had had to co-sign, with Jack Lustig, a performance evaluation which put the kid on probation. From then on, it had been all downhill.

But now I too am one of the bad boys, thought Bradford. Suppose the little dildo had intended some kind of half-assed gesture? Sympathy, solidarity, something like that. What would be the effect of getting your nose busted by somebody to whom you'd made such an offering? Pure, final hatred. And Wilson was capable of serious violence. Bradford had no doubt about it. Wilson was also the sort who would always get it wrong. He would blow himself up, like Mr. Verloc. Or, like the morons of Oklahoma City, blow up the wrong people—clerks, typists, janitors, kids in day care. Or me, Bradford thought. I am definitely one of the wrong people.

Suddenly, there was nothing funny about it. He realized he was afraid.

He went upstairs and took his father's .38 from a bureau drawer. It was an old weapon, gleaming blue steel, with rubber Pachmeyer grips. The sheer dead weight of it always surprised him, made him wonder if he could hold it steady, aim and fire with any accuracy. The doubt was not reasonable. He was much stronger than most.

Loading the pistol, putting it into the drawer of his bedside table, he felt futile and still a bit frightened. If Wilson decided to come for him with a weapon, he wasn't likely to show up at the house.

By bedtime Bradford had decided he was being paranoid. Probably. The trouble with fights was, you never knew when they were over.

On Tuesday after seventh period, he was straightening up his desk when Molly came in. Today she wore a denim jacket and overalls baggy enough to make her exquisite southern parts less apparent than usual. Her long hair was drawn up and bound near the top of head, falling in a fan-shape over her right shoulder.

"Hey," said Bradford. "I hear you were sick."

"Big-time."

"You okay now?'

"Mostly." She set her backpack on one of the student desks. Stood beside it, looking ill at ease.

"I read about what happened to you. I'm really sorry."

"Me too. But it's not the end of the world. Not unlike a bad case of the flu, actually."

"Worse than that."

He gazed at her and was reminded of kindergarten classmates: girls whose mothers never cut their hair. Ultra feminine dolls in gingham or cotton, thick tresses to the waists.

"I was going to call you," she said. "But you're not in the book."

"I'll give you the number." That was it. Dolly hair.

She put her hands behind her and leaned against the doorframe.

"I also wrote you a letter. Which I tore up."

"I wish you hadn't."

"Why are they picking on you?"

"I am perceived as being . . . unfriendly to minority students."

"You treat everybody the same. I saw that when I worked for you."

"That's the terrible injustice. I am mean to everyone, regardless of race, creed, or color."

"Are you depressed?"

"A little," lied Bradford, who was trying to will away an incipient erection. "But look--I have a job."

"Still."

"I appreciate the sympathy."

"I have another reason for being here."

"Which is?"

"You owe me a ride home."

"I certainly do."

That does it, he thought.

Molly lived in Pacific Heights. Before they reached the car, Bradford knew the exact route he would take. Entering the Presidio, he hung a left onto West Pacific.

"You're going the wrong way."

"The hell I am."

Bradford parked where the dog-walkers did, in a tree-shaded dirt lot just east of Julius Kahn playground. It was still early, though, and there was only one other car.

"Come here."

71

Molly sat straight, hands on her thighs, as if poised to get out of the car. She closed her eyes and murmured something he couldn't hear. Then he heard her seatbelt click, and she slid toward him. Kissing her, he felt that losing the job, everything bad that had ever happened to him, was proper payment for just this.

After a minute of tongues and lips, Bradford said, "You brushed your teeth."

"In the girls'. I got some weird looks."

More kissing.

"What are you doing?"

"Unbuttoning your button."

He slid his hand inside the overalls and down her belly. She convulsed as if shocked or burned. With his right arm he held her tight but felt her strength, knew she might break his grip. So he begged.

"Please. Please."

She had turned her face away, but then turned back, not looking at him, and pressed her face against his neck and collarbone, as if ashamed. Bradford found what he wanted, moved a finger gently, rhythmically.

She raised her head once again. More kissing. She began to rock, matching his rhythm, and suddenly stretched out, curved like a bow, her face above his now, thrown back. She cried out once, twice. She stretched herself again and again, feet braced against the floor.

When she was quiet, collapsed against him, he said, "That was a pretty good one."

"I feel like an animal."

"In a sense, we're all—"

"--Bullshit." She sat up straight, looked around. "Did anybody see?"

"No."

"Are you sure?"

"Yes."

Molly put her hand down the overalls and grimaced, as if adjusting tight underwear. She withdrew the hand and looked grimly at her fingertips.

"Am I deflowered?"

"No!"

"There's no blood."

"I was never inside."

She buttoned the overalls, sat up straight, looked ahead into the woods. She sighed. "I may not have it anyway. Female jocks deflower themselves a lot."

Bradford licked his fingertips, absently.

"What are you <u>doing</u>?"

"Tasting your pussy."

"Oh, gross!"

"Not at all."

After a moment she said, "Were you just playing on my sympathy?"

"No."

Silence.

"Molly, I've been obsessed with you for a year. You know that."

"You said you <u>weren't</u> obsessed."

"Call it second-degree obsession." Bradford drew her close, kissed her cheek. "I've scarcely thought of any female but you. Haven't touched any but you."

"Really?"

"Yes!" In the moment Bradford realized that the statement was absolutely true. The fact made him happy.

"So what do we do now?"

"Become lovers."

"Right this minute."

"Soon."

"But I'm <u>underage</u>."

"I don't care, and neither do you."

"Where would we see each other?"

73

"My place, mostly. But maybe we could do weekend trips."

"No. I couldn't. My mother knows everybody, and everybody knows me. We'd have to go to Iceland."

"My place then. Till you graduate."

Still facing the woods, Molly closed her eyes. "I really like you, you know. I'm not on some power trip."

"Power trip?"

"There's this girl that's slept with two teachers, one in middle school, one at Hamilton. We have these discussions at lunch about whether she should destroy their lives."

"Wow. And I thought I knew what was going on."

"If we do it, will you be afraid of me?"

"I don't think so. In the last ten minutes I've done enough to get myself a year in the slammeroo."

"Listen. I'm going to ask you something weird. But I want a serious answer, because you're in a position to know."

"Ask away."

"If Stanford or some Ivy League school found out I was involved with you, would that hurt my chances? Of getting in, I mean."

"Hell, no. You'd belong to a chic minority. Sexually abused females."

"This isn't funny to me."

"I'm not sure it's a joke. Anyway, they almost certainly wouldn't find out; but if they did, they wouldn't care. They're much more interested in your jump shot than your sex life."

"You think so?"

"I know so. Whatever gave you such an idea?"

"I read about that girl that Harvard dumped. The one who killed her mother."

Bradford gazed at her, uncomfortably reminded of how young she was. At last he said, "The cases are not at all comparable."

"I hope not. Look, I have to get home."

Bradford started the car, headed back toward the Masonic Gate.

"Come to my place this weekend."

"I need to think."

"We won't set a time. I'll be there all weekend."

"Too much pressure."

"You need to know that it matters to me."

She made him stop a block from her house, then leaned over and kissed him. She drew back slightly, looked into his eyes. "I wouldn't marry you, you know. Or live with you. I'm going to college."

"Okay." The dolly hair tickled his face.

"Really?"

"You make the rules."

"Goodnight."

"Yes."

SEVEN

The next morning Bradford looked for Molly at school but did not see her. Her name did not appear on the absentee bulletin delivered to his classroom at mid-day. During his preparation period he went to the office and looked up her schedule, then peeped through the window of her calculus classroom. There she was, in the second row, hand raised. It seemed odd to him that she could put her mind to mathematics after what had happened the day before. He felt she ought to be gazing out the window, or down at her desk, in an attitude of distraction or meditation.

When the day was over, he waited for her in his classroom, but she did not come. At three-forty-five he locked his door and went downstairs to see Joe Hensley. The Colonel had pulled his shades and was at his desk, marking exams in the yellowish light of overhead globes. He beckoned to Bradford, who went over and sat down in the student's desk directly before his old mentor. Bradford took the broadside from his inside pocket, handed it over.

The Colonel unfolded the paper, looked at it, and smiled.

"Ones and twos," he said, deepening his bass in satire. He was known for occasional Darth Vader imitations.

"You've heard of them."

"I got this about two months ago."

"I was wondering if Wilson could have sent it. It was postmarked the day before our little . . . encounter."

The Colonel looked at Bradford. "You seem a bit obsessed with him. Remember, he's just a country boy. However rowdy and bigoted."

"Who else, then?"

"Well—offhand--I see two possibilities. Someone else who knows us and knows we're conservatives. Or somebody who read about the Shabazz business in the papers."

"Where'd they get our addresses? I'm not in the phone book."

"That can't be too difficult."

Bradford nodded.

The Colonel touched the paper with his fingertips. "Does this appeal to you?"

"When I'm pissed off."

"As you have reason to be." The Colonel shut off his desk lamp, and his face became shadowy. "I've thought a good deal about your situation. As I think you know. I have literally lost sleep over it."

"I'm sorry to hear that."

"I try to imagine what I would have done in such circumstances, and I find it very difficult. This simply could not have happened when I was your age."

"You had your own challenges."

"Of course. But they were relatively simple. War came. I went. Everybody supported me."

"At least nobody's shooting at me."

The Colonel picked up the broadside, read. "What strikes me about this," he said at last, "is its simplicity and logic. Its literacy. Though perhaps the tone is a bit hysterical."

"A bit."

"Still—not at all the usual Klan rant. Wouldn't you agree? As an English teacher?"

"Yeah."

"If they're serious, and principled, I could respect them."

"Principled how?"

"In observing the Geneva Conventions. Sparing women, children, and the apolitical."

"Hey. Pretty shocking, coming from a teacher of civics."

"I am also a teacher of history."

"Meaning?"

"That movements of this sort are sometimes just and necessary."

"Things are that bad."

"I keep telling myself they may not be. That nobody should make a judgment based on what's happening in San Francisco. This . . . lint screen for the detritus of a culture."

"But they might be."

"In my bones I feel a real smash-up coming. And to be quite cold-blooded about it, maybe better now than later."

"Race war."

"Yes."

"Wow."

"Give me an example, please, of a modern society which has peacefully resolved the competing claims of large racial and ethnic groups."

"Uh-huh."

"No 'uh-huhs.' Think about it. I keep hoping I've missed one."

Bradford considered, then said, "Point taken."

78

"In my view, we're thirty years behind the former Yugoslavs. You have civil war there because there is no strong majority, only a plurality, and the largest group isn't strong enough to suppress or assimilate the others. Here we are still the majority. If the flashpoint comes soon, we might have victory instead of stalemate or defeat."

"What would victory be like?"

"It's probably too late for repatriation. Maybe the country could be partitioned. On our terms."

"Alabama and Georgia for the blacks, New Mexico and Arizona for the Latinos."

"Something like that."

The Colonel handed the broadside to Bradford. "One would prefer, of course, that the majority would simply see the wisdom of preventing brutes of all races, including our own, from bringing children into the world. With fewer and better people, and with the current racial balance maintained, we might be able to settle our differences. But—given our gross sentimentality about baby-making—that's not likely to happen."

"Well. Shall I join up?"

"Only if you can't stand the way things are. Or will become."

Bradford waved the paper. "I keep thinking they're not for real."

"If not, others—elsewhere—are. And, if you buy the argument, it doesn't matter. You're morally obligated to go out, even on your own, and make nasty calls or smash faces."

"You win."

"Just teasing. You don't really have the . . . temperament for this sort of thing, do you?"

"I don't know."

The Colonel made a small gesture of dismissal, as if—perhaps—he did not care to be misunderstood. "You're not

79

political. You enjoy the rest of life too much. Sports, women. Books."

"At the moment I'm not enjoying much of anything."

The Colonel spoke slowly and distinctly. "Do nothing in haste."

Bradford saw Molly in the hallways but nowhere else. Each time she acknowledged him by raising her hand slightly, wiggling her fingers.

So that his house would be impeccable, he had his cleaning lady work an extra day at the end of that week. He purchased new sheets, pillows, and pillowcases. At Walgreen's he bought KY Jelly, Spray'nWash, and a package of sheepskin condoms, the only kind he could endure.

On Saturday morning he was up and dressed at seven, and by noon he had marked more than half of the week's essays. After lunch he checked his cupboards and fridge, made a list, and called it in to the gourmet grocery he used whenever a lady friend was coming to call. The goods were delivered at three. By four he had nearly finished his papers and was feeling quite edgy. He needed to go downstairs and hit the bag, but he didn't want to be sweaty when she arrived; so instead he watched college football on ESPN. He put off dinner until nearly eight; and at nine, when he was sure she wasn't coming, he put on his old copy of *True Grit* and got slightly drunk.

On Sunday morning he cured his mild hangover by punching the bag. After breakfast, using a clipboard and binder paper, he did some desultory lesson planning and then picked up the Sunday paper. With fascination he read a story about a coal mine fire which had been burning for twenty years and was getting worse. For a long time smoke had risen only from the main shaft, but now the fire had spread underground. In the town nearby smoke came out of sewers and old wells. Gas seeped into basements, and people got sick.

When he finished lunch, he began to feel that Molly was not coming and, breaking a resolution, he had two bloody marys, after which he brushed his teeth and chewed a breath mint for good measure. He watched the 49ers for a while—he was a fan, and they were playing well—but eventually lost interest. He went upstairs, lay down, but didn't sleep. From four until nearly seven he paced the house and rehearsed, mostly in his mind but sometimes aloud as well, the intelligent and subtly seductive things he would say to her. At last he ate a sandwich, drank half a bottle of wine, and watched *Sixty Minutes*. At eight-thirty he turned off the set, got his jacket, and headed for Dullea's.

EIGHT

In Cole Valley the street was ugly with the trash of weekend revels. There was a dry rustle of windblown paper and cardboard, the tinkle of a rolling bottle. Fog tumbled past <u>Dullea's</u> in green neon, beneath which a leprechaun, also green, lifted a glass over and over.

The place was nearly empty when Bradford entered. A young couple, their faces a foot apart, hunched at a corner table. They had the sad and earnest look of people beginning a quarrel or making one up. Two old men sat at the end of the bar, talking to the weekend man, whom Bradford didn't know. He took a stool at the other end, ordered a boilermaker.

When the bartender brought the mug and the tiny conical glass, Bradford let them sit for a few minutes, to prove he wasn't desperate. At last he gulped the shot, felt the streak of fire in his esophagus, then the gentler expanding heat in his stomach. He took half the beer in one swallow, greasy and tasteless, and then considered a yellowing sign stuck in one corner of the bar mirror. Our credit manager is Helen Wait. If you want credit, go to Helen Wait. At fourteen he had found this immensely funny.

To his left, the lamps above the pool tables were dark. On June 12, 1982, he had run the table closest to the front, winning eighty-six dollars. He had not played in years.

He studied his glum face in the mirror and gave desultory thought to his options. One more, walk home, okay in the morning. Three more, walk home, tough out a hangover. Get tanked, call a cab, call in sick.

The choice made, he was looking at his third chaser when he felt a hand on his shoulder.

"Mr. Bradford."

Wilson, a chevron of white bandage covering his nose. Bradford stared at him.

The kid had been looking down and away, but now he met Bradford's gaze, held it a moment. His eyes were that pure arctic blue, verging on rage or hilarity. He spoke too rapidly.

"The Colonel says I was an asshole. Miss Janie too. So I guess I was. I apologize." Again he looked away, but held out his hand.

Bradford shook it, with misgivings. "I wish I'd be been there when Janie called you an asshole."

Wilson snickered. "She didn't use that word."

Suddenly he stepped aside, gestured toward a man who stood a few feet behind him.

"Somebody wants to meet you. Harley Briscoe."

The man stepped forward, shook hands. He was about Bradford's age but taller, stooped with that scoliotic thickening of back and shoulders that one sees in teamsters. He had thinning blond hair, combed straight back, and a mustache.

"A pleasure."

"Yes, Sir," said Briscoe. "For me too." He took the stool beside Bradford. Wilson sat beside Briscoe. When the bartender came, they ordered draft beer.

"Read about your problems."

"Uh huh."

"Also, I remember you from high school."

"Jimmy D. said you played ball."

"Second string. At Lincoln. Before the Hamilton game, we had a sign up in the locker room. 'Stop Bradford.'"

"Which you did, as I recall."

"I think we doubled-teamed you."

Bradford nodded.

"So how you holdin' up?"

Bradford hesitated. The question seemed presumptuous. "I feel like I'm being double teamed."

In the bar mirror Bradford saw Briscoe smile and nod. He had a boney face with a big nose and strong cheekbones. His high, shiny forehead seemed flat in places, like a faceted gem.

"I'll be at that Board of Ed meeting," he said. "Me and some others. You think you'll get your job back?"

"No."

Again Briscoe nodded. "There's this rumor that Bob Shapley called the Feds and asked for an investigation of Hamilton."

"Really."

"That's what I hear."

"Who from?"

"This floosie I know. I can't tell you her name. Shapley's her hairdresser."

"Okay."

Bradford thought about Bob Shapley, who was the gay vote on the Board. He was the loosest of cannons, and even his allies did not always take him seriously. He struck Bradford as the sort who had gone through life behaving badly and never getting paid back. The sort whose parents did not believe in corporal punishment. The sort who stayed close to the yard teacher during recess and treated the housekeeper's children badly because they couldn't retaliate. In Bradford's experience the great majority of such people were women; but there were occasional exceptions.

After a moment he said, "It doesn't worry me particularly. I'm so innocent I'm unframable."

"Nobody's that innocent."

"I am. I'm numero uno on Santa's list of who's nice."

Silence. Bradford considered his remarks, found them fatuous. He realized he was drunk.

"Listen, Mr. Bradford. Come for a ride with us. I have a proposition for you."

Bradford looked at his watch. "Nine-thirty on a Sunday night is a lousy time for a proposition. Or anything else."

"On the contrary. Good because unexpected."

"So make it here."

"We need privacy."

Bradford laughed, looked around. The young couple had gone. "Two old drunks and a sleepy bartender."

"It's just good policy. Wynn and I'll drive around a little. You start for home and we'll pick you up."

"You know I'm walking."

"Just happened to see you. We'll go now. You leave in five minutes."

"Hey. I have to go to work tomorrow."

"We all do. You'll be home by eleven."

Briscoe and Wilson left. Neither had touched his beer. The bartender would remember. Bradford ordered another boilermaker. He considered the possibility that Wilson had enlisted Briscoe to help beat the shit out of him. Even kill him.

Melodrama. Still, not out of the question. He would watch them every second, and if they gave him the slightest shit, he would go for them. Take out one with a kick to the groin, finish the other with his fists. Beat them to fucking death.

Breaking Wilson's nose had not been nearly enough.

Bradford tossed a twenty on the bar, walked out. He headed up Cole, looking for them. The scutter of blown trash was steady now, along with a lowing wind from far above. The only person on the street was a crazed homeless man whose small rosy face nestled in a curly mass of beard and mustache. Over and over he threw a wad of paper up the sidewalk and then chased it, laughing in innocent delight.

Two of them, thought Bradford. Possibly armed.

He found them waiting two blocks away, Briscoe at the wheel, Wilson in back.

"Hey, there!" said Briscoe as Bradford got in beside him. "Glad you decided to join us."

Bradford sat a bit sideways so that his peripheral vision would register Wilson's movements. Briscoe started the car, made a U-ee.

"You live on States Street, right?"

"Yeah."

"Where we're going is near there. That's why you won't be out late."

Bradford did not reply.

"What's it like," asked Briscoe, "living around all the faggots?"

Bradford was used to the question, and he made the standard reply. "It's not a problem. They're great for property values."

"I've heard that," said Briscoe. He glanced Bradford, his eyes brown and watchful. Like Molly's but bigger and brighter. "What about <u>seeing</u> them all the time? Hearing them."

Bradford thought for an answer. It was in fact the girly voices that he detested, but he would not give Briscoe the satisfaction.

"I don't see them much. On my stretch of the street they're not a majority, and I don't shop on Castro."

Briscoe went over the hill on Clayton, took a right on Market, then the sharp switchback to Eighteenth. Halfway up the hill on Eureka, he pulled into a stop for the 35 bus, killed the engine and lights.

"Okay, Mr. Bradford. Here's what we have in mind."

Briscoe leaned forward to see clearly between the wheel and the rear-view mirror, then pointed. "Shapley's place is the third on the right. That's his BMW right out front. After a little detour, I'm gonna pull alongside, and somebody's gonna put a bullet through the driver's side window."

Briscoe put a fingertip to his temple. "At about this height. Tomorrow morning somebody else will call him at his shop and tell him that the next time, he'll be in the driver's seat. Clear so far?"

Bradford nodded.

"Nobody will mention you or your situation. But we'll stop Shapley cold."

"You think so."

"Yeah. He's a yellow coward. Somebody did a little number on him about a year ago, and he kept quiet for a long time. Now I guess he needs a reminder."

Bradford recalled that, in truth, Shapley had not been much in the news lately.

"You belong to Ones and Twos?"

Briscoe turned toward him. The brown eyes gleamed, appeared to threaten. Then softened. "If you got the statement in the mail, which is how most people hear about them, you know I might not tell you if I was."

Bradford said nothing..

"My proposition, Mr. Bradford, is that you take the shot."

"You're already two. Why sign me on?"

"Forget that stuff. The scum have hurt you, bad. Do this, and you begin to get even."

Briscoe started the car, drove off.

"I'm gonna drive a wide circle, kill some time. Then we go by, do the job. You don't want to play, we drop you at your place first. Just one thing: you keep quiet about this. Absolutely quiet."

Wilson spoke for the first time since Dullea's. "Gut-check time, Mr. B.."

Bradford turned around. "You little ding-dong. You want somethin' else broken?"

"Ready when you are, Stud!"

"Nobody is fighting anybody tonight."

Something in the tone made Bradford glance at Briscoe. He held up a small automatic pistol, as if to warn them both. Bradford had no idea where it had come from. After a moment Briscoe slipped it into his jacket pocket.

Five minutes later, as he approached States, he spoke again.

"Okay. You want out, Mr. Bradford?"

Bradford said nothing.

Heading up Eureka, Briscoe took the pistol from his pocket, offered it to Bradford.

After a moment Bradford held out his hand, palm up. He shifted the weapon to his right hand, and the passenger side window came whirring down.

"Remember. About temple-high."

When Briscoe stopped, Bradford extended his arm, and sighted on the window. Then he swung the arm down and to the right. He fired twice into the gas tank. Briscoe let out the clutch and the car lurched forward. Bradford had to turn, stretch, and lean out the window to stay on target.

The third shot blew the tank. Sudden heat scorched Bradford's hand, forearm, one side of his face.

"Fucking shit!" screamed Wilson.

The car roared up Eureka. Briscoe hit a right on Twenty-third, then another on Noe, slowing down.

When they reached Market, he looked at Bradford and grinned. He was sweating.

"If I hadn't pulled away, 'n if that tank'd been full, we'd'a gone up too."

Bradford touched the side of his face. It felt sunburned.

"I never thought of that."

NINE

At home the sameness of things surprised him. Old stairs creaking in the usual places, the hum of his ancient alarm clock. Hangers jangling in the closet as he put away his jacket. He undressed, put on pajamas. Alone in stressful times he often talked to himself, but now he was silent, conscious of his own breathing. At last he went back downstairs, drank a quarter-glass of straight bourbon, then went to bed. He lay on his side, with only the sheet covering him, the right side of his face still hot from the blast. He did not expect to sleep, but did.

Waking at six, he lay still and thought of calling in sick, getting tanked again. He had not taken a day off in more than a year and was certainly entitled. But when he got up to pee he felt not at all sick or hung over. Perhaps the act had purged some poisons; though that notion seemed romantic. Yet life gave strange remissions, periods of undeserved and unexpected strength. He shaved, dressed, went downstairs. He was spooning coffee into a Melitta filter when he noticed a bottle of Jack Daniels on the kitchen table. He stared at it, the hand with the spoon stopped in mid-air, until he remembered. At four o'clock he had come downstairs and drunk two doubles. So life had given nothing; he was still tanked. After toast and coffee he went back upstairs and brushed his teeth again. On the way to school he chewed breath mints.

Approaching the front steps, he noted uncommon activity among the kids who congregated there before the first class. Heads together--he thought of barbershop quartets-- they studied the morning paper, and Bradford went cold with the sudden belief that they were reading about what he had done. The police could be waiting at his classroom door. This conjecture became near certainty when, as he entered the mailroom, three teachers stopped talking and looked at him.

"He doesn't know," said Dennis Byrne. "I can tell by the angelic expression."

"Know what?"

Dennis took a folded newspaper from under his arm. "Read it and weep."

"Just tell me."

"We're history. The Supe is closing us down."

Bradford read. According to an unnamed source, the Superintendent was to announce, that very evening, plans to close Hamilton and two other schools. The buildings would be ceded to the city and turned into homeless shelters. Bradford had to set his jaw to keep from grinning in relief.

His first class seemed to go well. He did not trust the perception; and during the second, another self stood to one side, observed the proceedings. His speech was distinct, if a trifle slower than usual. The kids were interested, the discussion focused and productive. Perhaps, he thought, I should be drunk all the time. During his prep period he searched the paper for something about the burning of the car; but found nothing. He remembered Briscoe's judgment of Shapley and hoped the man had been too terrified to report the incident.

But as students were arriving for his third period class, he recalled, with yet another chill, that tonight his colleagues were to speak on his behalf, urge his reinstatement. The irony was gross and sobering; and in his last two classes he paced, stumbled over words. His gestures were like tics, and he made the kids nervous.

After school there was an *ad hoc* meeting of teachers to discuss strategy in opposing the Superintendent. By then Bradford had a full-blown hangover. He wanted only to go home, go to bed; but the prospect of being the subject of public speech appalled him. He had to stop them if he could.

He sat at the back of the room, hands tightly clasped on the desk before him. Though he planted his feet flat on the floor, his knees shook now and then. Just before adjournment he begged, haltingly, that in view of the crisis his colleagues postpone appeals on his behalf and devote all their energy to saving the school. Stuttering a bit, he said that he was perfectly happy to be teaching once more.

Apparently no one believed him.

"It hurt all of us, Mickey," said Dennis, gently. "Not just you."

Bradford opened his mouth to reply: *they've got something on me that you don't know about.* But the words would not come.

On his way home he stopped for the afternoon paper, in which he found two paragraphs about the burning of Shapley's car. They contained no speculation about cause or perpetrators. Making his left onto States Street, Bradford again expected to find the police waiting. They were not. In the kitchen he drank enough bourbon to take the edge off his miserable hangover, then lay down. At five he rose, made himself a sandwich of bologna and stale bread, drank three beers, and considered the enormity of his eventual humiliation. At seven, noon, six and eleven the local TV news would recount his cruelty to Shabazz, his firing, his revenge, and the dreadful irony of his colleagues defense of him. Few if any of them would ever speak to him again.

He thought of going back to bed, of getting tanked again. He thought of his father's .38. and then of a length of hose in his basement that he might attach to the exhaust pipe of his car.

Play-acting. Whatever was done to him, others would do.

At six-thirty he brushed his teeth and set off for the meeting. On the way he chewed more breath mints and had a surprising but fragile sense of injustice. He could not help feeling that what he had done was not all that terrible.

The central office of the school district was located in the buildings of a high school which had been closed for thirty years. Bradford parked in a lot across the street and was weaving his way through a procession of people when an unpleasant odor caused him to look up and clearly see them: the fucking homeless, marshaled for the meeting by their various advocates and caretakers. A sudden wind whipped their ponchos and overcoats, their dry and matted hair. Bradford loathed them.

The ancient auditorium was as dark as a movie theater. Most of the old ceiling lights were out, and those still lit were sparse, outsized stars. On either side of the stage, set into the plaster walls, black-rimmed, white-faced clocks were barely readable. One was stopped forever at eight-forty-five, the other running three hours behind. On stage in a bloom of white light stood a long, curving structure of blond wood, rather like a judicial bench, behind which sat the Board members. The whole set-up, Bradford had often thought, was demeaning; it made the audience somehow captive and subservient. Kids at a school assembly.

Bradford entered during the pledge to the flag, a sustained mumbling. When it was over, he found Janie, Dennis, Joe and some others; they had saved him an aisle seat. When the Board President called the first speaker, a stately blonde in a white shift and high heels ran clippety-clop to the mike.

"Honored Commissioners, Mr. Superintendent, members of the audience. I am here tonight to speak to you about monosodium glutamate."

Laughter, in trickles. Which joined in a stream, then a torrent.

The woman shouted to be heard. "Every day, in every school cafeteria, the children of this district are compelled—compelled—to ingest great amounts of this potentially deadly—"

The Board President beat a fierce rhythm with her gavel, called for order.

And so it went all evening. For every relevant speaker there was another whose hobby horse had to be malleted to death. Bradford grew sober and edgy. He learned which of his colleagues were to speak on his behalf, and twice he rose and crept about, stepping on feet and crouching in aisles, begging them in whispers not to raise the issue of his removal. To his relief, they relented, agreed.

John Rohrer and two ed school profs, one each from Stanford and Berkeley, spoke in favor of the Superintendent's plan. Boos and hisses interrupted them. As each finished and turned away from the mike, he evoked a single comment from the darkness at the rear. The man from Stanford had a high voice, and someone called him a cunt. Another voice told the Berkeley man to get his Commie ass back to the People's Republic. A third called Rohrer a little piece of shit. Bradford, remembering Winnie-the-Pooh,

94

whispered, "That's just what I think myself!" But the rowdies gave him no real comfort. Tonight they had taken the enemy by surprise. Next time the left would be out in force.

Thereafter he lost interest in the formal proceedings. One of the voices had sounded familiar. The others he had not heard before, but he had no doubt that the remarks had been orchestrated. Despite the darkness he turned to look back and each time someone returned his gaze. Bradford knew perhaps half the people in the audience, but the men who looked back at him were strangers.

Briscoe's pals.

Or cops.

Speakers came and went for nearly an hour more, surreal figures halved from head to toe by the beam of a ceiling spot, one side afire, the other dark. A tall young man in a camouflage jacket excoriated Hamilton. He had a black beret covered with political buttons, and well before he had finished, a ball-game chant arose in the pitch black rear of the auditorium.

"Bullshit, bullshit, bullshit!"

Next came an eminent alumnus, a founding partner of a huge and obscenely successful law firm. He called the Superintendent's proposal an outrage and spoke at length of his formative experience as stroke oar on the 1949 Hamilton crew. The crowd noise grew louder, coughs and grunts and laughs and syllables and clumping feet, raising in Bradford's mind the image of a flow of junk, as if some cornucopic dump truck poured garbage endlessly into a landfill.

The last speaker was Jenifer Sharp's mother.

"My daughter's about to graduate from Hamilton. She has friends there, and she's had some good experiences. But she's had bad ones too. I have to say that for some teachers and administrators, whatever an African-American child does just isn't good enough. It's time we had equal educational opportunity in San Francisco, and Alexander Hamilton doesn't measure up to that goal."

"Fat, stupid bitch."

"Now, now," said Janie.

"Fat, stupid bitch."

"'Dey eats dere pain.'"

"What?"

"Never mind."

Shortly before ten, as the Board began its discussion, the lights went out. There was a chorus of ohs.

The Board President shouted to be heard. "Would everybody just sit tight? We'll see if we can solve the problem."

A rumble of talk arose. Soon the President spoke again. "Those of you in the back, would you open the doors and see if we can get some light from the street?"

This was done, with little effect. On the far right there was the sound of a scuffle. A man cried out.

Bradford took Janie's arm. "Let's get out of here."

But the aisle was already full. Bradford put an arm around Janie. Someone large pushed past him, and he threw an elbow, felt it hit bone. The someone cried out, and for a moment Bradford felt better than he had all day.

Outside he and Janie walked halfway up the block. Eventually the others found them, Joe, Dennis, Lucille Graham.

"What was that about?" asked Lucille.

No one answered. In the chilly night Bradford suddenly felt himself losing it, beginning to tremble. He set his jaw and folded his arms. He stiffened his legs to keep his knees from shaking. One after another, the nasty possibilities came to him: jail, humiliation, the loss of Molly and the revenge of Wynn Wilson.

The Englishman in the camouflage jacket stumbled by. He had his face in his hands, and between the fingers there was blood. A weeping woman held his arm.

A half block away someone with a bullhorn announced that the meeting would resume on the following Monday night. Bradford and Hensley escorted the women to their cars, and Bradford found he could barely walk. Stepping off curbs, he came down stiff-legged, jarring himself. He tripped over a curb and nearly fell.

When the women were gone, the Colonel looked down at him.

"Are you drunk?"

"H-hung over."

"Booze is not the answer, Young Fella."

"No."

"Pull yourself together."

"Yeah."

As he unlocked his car in the lot, two long shadows approached.

Here it comes, he thought. Whatever it is.

But when the men reached his car they went on by, turning their heads to grin at him. One held up a clenched fist.

"Hang in there, Buddy. We're with you."

"We stopped that shit," said the other, "and we'll stop the rest of it."

Bradford had withdrawn his key from the lock. He stood quite still, watching as the two men got into an old car two aisles over.

He had no idea who they were.

TEN

Bradford stood at the black formica counter in the kitchen and poured himself a double shot. He stared at the red hand of the kitchen clock as it moved from five to eleven. He poured the stuff back into the bottle, spilling some, and went down to the garage. He draped his jacket over the warm hood of the car, rolled up his sleeves, and began hitting the bag without gloves. Each effort set off a small spasm in his arm and shoulder, made the blows palsied and weak. After four rounds he was sick and stood for several minutes over one of the gray and grimy cement washtubs, expecting to puke. When the nausea passed, he went two more rounds, until his knuckles bled. He climbed the stairs to the kitchen, drank one shot, and went upstairs to bed.

The next day his classes went badly. At the end of third period he had a visit from Jesse Martinez, his successor as assistant principal. Martinez said he had a probation officer wanting to talk to somebody who knew Rickey Bradford.

"I know it's not your problem any more. I didn't promise him anything."

For weeks Bradford had been refusing such requests; but now, without knowing quite why, he took the pink <u>While You Were Out</u> slip from Martinez's hand.

"You're not . . . related to the kid, are you?"

"Joined fast at the hip," said Bradford. "Mickey and Rickey."

At lunchtime, as he dialed the number from a cubicle in the Counseling Center, he felt not only regret but something oddly like dread. As if he were touching bases with a girlfriend whose period was late.

"Hey, thanks for calling. You know this kid pretty well?"

"As well as anybody here. Which isn't saying much."

"No relation, I assume."

"All us Bradfords were on the Mayflower."

The man laughed softly. "Got anything good to say about him?"

"Not really. What's he done now?"

"Looks like he sold a rock to a kid at Luther Burbank. I may have to send him down."

"Uh huh."

"I mean really down. Not just to the ranch."

"I see."

"What can you tell me?"

"Last year he was busted for dealing at the Wharf. But you probably know about that."

"Yeah."

"Out here, a year ago October, a teacher observed what she thought was a transaction. A month later I did the same. But we never caught him with the goods."

"Oh . . . kay."

"Then in January we found a little girly stoned on weed in one of the bathrooms. While under the influence she told us she'd bought the stuff from our pal. The next day, with

Daddy and his lawyer in tow, she recanted. Said she didn't know the dealer."

"Uh-huh."

"So—no hard evidence."

"I hear you." There was a pause. "He got any chance to graduate?"

"He'd have to pass every course."

"But he could?"

"Yeah."

"You wouldn't bet on it."

"I wouldn't bet, period."

"Really."

"Yeah."

"Okay. Thanks for your time."

In the cafeteria at lunch Bradford sat alone, eating mashed potatoes and mystery meat, remembering the day he'd almost nailed his young namesake. From his office window he'd caught sight of Rickey Bradford in the center of the courtyard. There seemed no reason for his being precisely there. A chubby boy approached, spoke. Rickey Bradford reached into his pocket and withdrew a small object which glinted in the sunlight. Cellophane. The chubby boy examined it, handed it back, and began to dig in his front pocket. In a matter of perhaps eight seconds Bradford went through the outer office, around a corner, down a short passage. As he burst through double doors into the courtyard, Rickey Bradford had paper money in his left hand, but when he saw Mickey Bradford coming, he released the shiny object from his right. Bradford saw it bounce on the iron grate of a storm drain, fall through.

With the help of an irritated janitor Bradford spent much of that afternoon trying to remove the grate, but it was stuck or bolted. Not even a crowbar would budge it. Bradford called maintenance at the central office. Maintenance told him to call the Department of Public Works.

He did, and they promised to send a man out the next day. That night it rained heavily, and in the morning Bradford canceled the request.

Now Bradford thought about his conversation with the PO and thought he might have saved Rickey Bradford's ass. Literally. At the Woodson Vocational Institute, the state facility for which the kid was a candidate, older and harder lads would make regular and brutal use of that part of his anatomy. Of course the PO might send him down anyway.

The afternoon paper included an account of the trouble at the Board Meeting. The piece was mostly quotations. The Board President said that she would not yield to intimidation. Another Board member hinted that the lights had been sabotaged. The beaten Englishman compared the San Francisco to Mississippi in the sixties. The Superintendent spoke of a series of disturbing and "possibly related" events, including the "harassment" of an African-American assistant principal and the burning of a car belonging to Commissioner Shapley, who was known to favor the closing of the school. At lunch that day Bradford found that his colleagues regarded the evening as a public relations disaster.

Bradford taught through Wednesday, his work improving from poor to mediocre. That night he decided to take the rest of the week off. He called for a substitute, packed a bag, and called a cab. He stopped at the bank, withdrew five hundred dollars, and had the cabbie drop him at the Bridge Plaza, where he took a Golden Gate Transit bus to Stinson Beach. He checked into a hotel, using the name of Jay Berwanger, who in 1934 had been the first winner of the Heisman Trophy. For thirty-six hours Bradford stayed sober, ate, slept, walked and jogged on the beach. Late Friday afternoon he checked out and caught the bus back to the city. On the way he tried facing facts. For blowing the car he might get probation, but if Shapley sued, he could lose the house. He would certainly lose his job. Still, there were limits to what they could do to him. It was even possible that he might get away with it. Most criminals, after all, were never caught. His life was not over.

At eight that night his phone rang.

"Hello?"

"Mr. Bradford?"

He supposed the woman was selling something, but her cheery tone was welcome. It had been some time since any grown-up women had sounded truly glad to speak to him.

"Yes."

"You don't know me, but I've been asked to tell you that in a couple of days you'll get some news that will make you happy."

"Really."

"No foolin'. You have a good weekend now." The woman hung up.

Bradford collapsed into the recliner and brooded in the dark, without booze.

An hour later his doorbell rang, made him start.

Someone else.

On his way he thought of getting the old man's gun, confronting the intruder with it. Terrify the fucker. Make him admit every last diabolical motive.

It was Molly, in a down jacket and that skirt. In the foyer she kissed him lightly on the lips. He hugged her; kissed harder. In the thick jacket she seemed a giantess, more than he could handle.

"Where have you been?"

"I decided I wasn't coming near you till I was prepared."

"I haven't even seen you at school!"

"I didn't want you hassling me."

102

She allowed him to unzip and remove the jacket. He hung it in the closet; then embraced and kissed her again. She wore a white silk blouse and now seemed manageably smaller.

"It's cold in here."

"Sorry." He reached for the thermostat, turned it up. Then he lifted the skirt slightly, put his fingertips on the front of her thigh..

"Just hold me for a little."

He did. Her presence was a miracle, but soon the chaos of his recent life intruded, distracted. At last he said, "Prepared how?"

"I'm pilled. Totally safe."

"Jesus."

"I hope you appreciate it. That stuff has icky side effects."

"Of course I do. Where did you go?"

"Planned Parenthood. It takes a while to kick in, which is mainly why you haven't see me."

He led her to the kitchen, made hot tea. He understood that he would have to tell her everything. Could not proceed otherwise.

They faced each other across the kitchen table, and when he was done Molly ran a hand through her brassy hair, looked at him.

"That's unbelievable."

"Sort of."

"You think they'll catch you?"

"Maybe. Maybe not. That's not the issue."

"What is?"

"Whether we should go on with this."

"You don't want to?"

"Of course I want to."

She turned her head slightly, lifted her chin, gave him a sidelong look. "Like you said, it wouldn't be as bad as murdering my mother."

Bradford laughed. "Still."

"I never knew anybody who committed a crime."

"Probably you have. You just never knew anybody who confessed."

"If you mess with me, that'll be another one."

"Yeah. Though I'm not concerned about that."

"What are you concerned about?"

"Screwing up your life."

"You've sort of aleady done that."

"Not really. Not big-time."

In a moment her eyes glistened. "I have feelings for you."

Bradford reached, took her hand. "I know that. But everybody suffers that way, sooner or later. Messing with a criminal is a unique kind of trouble."

"What if I don't care?"

"You must care. The question is, what are you going to do. You need to think."

He got her some Kleenex. She blew her nose.

"Actually, I'm sort of glad to know you're not perfect."

Bradford laughed. "Was that a problem?"

"You always seem like you have it together. At school, anyway."

"Well. Now you know."

After a long pause she said, "Aren't you afraid?"

"A little."

"So am I."

"Of course. You just found out."

"God. I just don't know about this."

"You need to think."

"But if I decided to, you would. In spite of everything."

"Yes."

"Even though you're not sure it's a good idea."

"Yes. You know how I feel."

Molly said nothing.

"I had to tell you the truth. That's as far as I can go on moral principle."

"Oh." For the first time that evening, she had her wry look.

"There it is."

Now she gave him a look less wry than appraising. Then she stood up. "Okay. Where's a bedroom?"

"You want to sleep now? It's still pretty early."

"I want to be alone now. But I have to stay—my parents think I'm staying over at Anita's."

"All right. But you don't have to make up your mind tonight."

"I know that."

Bradford took her to the guest room. Pointed out the bathroom down the hall.

"Anything else you need?"

"No. Go away now."

Bradford started to close the door.

"Wait."

"What?"

"Do you know, I don't even know your name?"

"What?"

"I don't. The papers and stuff at school say your name is Michael. But I hear the teachers call you Mickey."

"It's Mickey."

"All right. Mickey."

Bradford went downstairs to turn out the lights, then lay down on his own bed. He left the door partly open.

Molly's arrival seemed a great joke. He considered and reconsidered each minute aspect of his absurdity, his humiliation. This took some time.

"Mickey."

Bradford awoke, stared at the vertical oblong of light between the door and the frame.

"Mickey. Where are you?"

He lurched from the bed, stumbled into the hall. Molly stood in the doorway to the guestroom. She wore a light green flannel nightgown. He went to her .

She put her arms around his neck, kissed him. Then said, "I don't care."

He took her hand, and they went to his room. She took off the nightgown, tossed it onto his bureau, and stood by the bed. As Bradford undressed, he saw that it was two o'clock. He had slept, and she had thought, for nearly three hours.

Molly turned back the covers and frowned. "You didn't make this bed!"

"Housekeeper. Friday's her day."

In bed she whispered, "You better not be hiding another woman."

"Not bloody likely."

They began the motions, but Bradford could not get an erection.

"It's okay," she said. "Do me with your hand."

"I have a better idea."

Bradford went down on her. In fifteen minutes she came twice.

"That was fantastic. What if I like it better?"

"Better than what?"

"Better than your thing."

Bradford sighed. "As of now, you have no basis for comparison."

"But what if I do? Would that make me a pervert?"

"If it did, you'd have plenty of company."

They slept. Bradford awoke at four with a piss hard-on. He went to the bathroom, waited for it to go down, and peed.

In bed he felt it coming back. When he was hard and knew he would remain so, he put on some lubricant, then gently rolled her over.

"What?"

"Now."

"Oh boy," she said.

He mounted, began to ease into her. There was a resistance of tissue. He pushed hard. It broke.

"Ouch!" said Molly.

He came quickly. Melted into her.

Before long she said, "Get off a minute, okay? Either I wet the bed or I'm bleeding to death."

She sat up, and Bradford turned on the bedside light. Molly leaned over, looked.

"I'm hemorrhaging!"

"No you're not. Lie down on my side."

Molly did as she was told. He got a clean washrag, wet it, gently washed her off.

"You're okay. The flow has stopped."

She got up, stared at the stain. As Bradford stripped the bed, she began to giggle.

"Aren't you going to leave it for the housekeeper?"

"Indeed not. My housekeeper has suffered certain reversals of fortune, but she is nonetheless a lady."

Molly began to laugh, could not stop. "Unlike . . . certain . . . people!"

She staggered to the bureau and took up the green nightgown. Slipped it over her head, let it fall, still laughing. Bradford took the sheets to the laundry chute. When he returned with fresh ones from the hall closet, he raised a forefinger.

"Such glee is most unseemly."

"You're going to wash away." Molly sniveled, caught her breath, blew her nose with tissue from the box on the nightstand. "My sacred virgin blood."

"Most certainly."

"Who are you being?"

"Herbert Marshall."

"Who's he?"

"British actor. Dead about a thousand years."

"Do another."

He shook his head. "The mood has passed. Besides, my range is limited. John Wayne, George Bush, Herbert Marshall."

"You're funny."

"I'm glad you think so, because you're going to need a sense of humor."

They went downstairs, drank hot chocolate, and ate stale oatmeal cookies. Back in bed, Bradford asked, "What made up your mind?"

"I just decided I was being chickenshit."

"Chickenshit."

"Yes. And I'm not that sort of person. Did you know I've been to survival school?"

"You have?"

"Yes. Like, they dump you in the wilderness and you have to take care of yourself."

"I've heard of it. And I'm impressed. Truly."

"So—what does it matter? I'm gonna do it with somebody, sooner or later. Right?"

"True."

"Besides, I'm a tough mother."

"What?"

"That's what my instructor said."

"In survival school."

"Yes."

Bradford rose early, drove to Noe Valley for sticky buns. When he returned, she was sitting up, reading the paper.

"I forgot to ask if you had any terrible diseases."

"I do not," said Herbert Marshall. "Do you?"

"No."

"Good."

"But God, I'm glad I went on that pill! If you knew how dumb most girls are about sex."

"I've heard the rumors," said Bradford, not Marshall.

"What are you going to do about the other thing? Your terrible crime."

"That's a very good question."

"Well?"

"I think . . . I think I'm going to see a lawyer."

"Makes sense to me. Did you ever think of just confessing?"

"Since you suggest it, I shall. Consider it, that is."

"You don't sound too enthusiastic."

"I guess I'm not. Mostly I just want to get away with it."

"I think you're too uptight for that."

"I'm not so sure. The other thing is, I'd rather not implicate the others, even though they're assholes."

"Would you have to?"

"Maybe not. A lawyer could tell me, I suppose."

"Ms. Shabazz and the politically correct. Do you really hate them?"

"I don't know. I don't like them."

"I think you should see the lawyer."

"All right. I will."

"Can I have another sticky bun?"

He gave her one. "This discussion has been very helpful."

"You're such a loner, any discussion would help."

"No. Just with you."

"That's very sweet, but I don't think it's true."

"I do."

"Mickey."

"What?"

"It's okay with me if you get away with it. But don't do anything else."

"I won't."

ELEVEN

Molly left at ten-thirty. The coach was running a Saturday practice.

"And I can't come tomorrow! I have a shitload of homework!"

As Bradford watched her stride off down States Street, he was smelling licorice from the straw-colored hillside across the street and realizing what he should have understood sooner. He would be only a part of her life, and perhaps one reason why his troubles did not greatly distress her was that her wager on him, if lost, would hardly break the bank. He told himself this was good.

She visited him for two hours in early evening on the following Wednesday. They fucked, came together.

"I must be this incredible slut. I like that even better."

"When I was your age, it was the ideal."

"You mean it's <u>dated</u>?"

"The belief in an ideal is dated. These days sex is supposed to be a smorgasbord. A little of this, a little of that."

"Cool. Where do you get the menu?"

"I have a couple of books I can give you. But I warn you. I'm a simple lad with simple tastes."

Molly took home *The Joy of Sex*, revised edition. When she returned on Sunday, she tossed it onto the small table in the foyer.

"That book is <u>weird</u>," she whispered, after a kiss.

"I'm sort of glad you think so."

For Bradford this remark was unleavened with irony. He wanted to run things in bed, and Molly seemed smaller in the missionary position. Between bouts they ate, read *The New York Times* and discussed current events. They played chess, at which she beat him, and Scrabble, at which he beat her. As he drove her home, Molly asked why he didn't want her to go down on him, putting quotation marks around the phrase.

"Never particularly enjoyed it. It's a sorry compromise between men desperate for sex and women desperate to avoid it."

"I thought it was <u>foreplay</u>."

Bradford shrugged.

"I think you're afraid of getting it bit off."

"Could be."

"But you like doing it to me."

"Love it."

"Why?"

"It's got something to do with getting back to where you came from. On some level, I hope you'll just swallow me up."

"Oooo! How gross! How uncool!"

"Sorry."

He did not tell her that he loved exciting her when he was not particularly excited himself. Or, for that matter, that he sometimes liked pumping her several seconds beyond the moment at which her pleasure became pain. All that she would understand in time. For now these and other truths would be his secret. His power.

He stopped at a corner a block from her house. As she opened the car door he asked, "What would your folks say, if they knew?"

Molly paused, thought about it. "They'd be happy I was screwing somebody male, 'cause they keep making these anxious little remarks about female jocks and lesbianism. They would not be happy that it's you."

"Uh-huh."

"Listen. Have you seen the lawyer?"

"I made an appointment, but he cancelled out on me."

"Reschedule."

"Okay."

"I mean it."

Bradford looked at her. "Bossy."

"I have to save you from yourself. In AP we're reading *Crime and Punishment*, and boy do I identify with that girl."

Bradford laughed. "You have a great and pure heart. Aside from that, you're the most un-Sonya-like female that ever lived."

"Maybe. But you really are Raskolnikov."

"Svidrigailov."

"No. Not really." She kissed his cheek. "See the lawyer, please."

Shortly after their first evening at his place, Bradford had called an attorney whose advertised specialty was representing cops and other public employees. The lawyer's name—much to Bradford's amusement--was Jerry Mason. Bradford made an appointment, but two days later he got a call from the man's secretary, whom he thought of as Bella Street. Bella said they'd have to reschedule because "Mr. M." had to be in court. When they had trouble finding a new and mutually agreeable time, Bradford had said he'd get back to her. Then he forgot to do so largely because, he knew perfectly well, he was simply hoping to get away with what he had done. But after Molly reminded him, he made another appointment..

Two days later, early in the morning, Jesse Martinez was waiting for him in the mailroom.

"There's some cop who wants to talk to you, in your old office. I'll handle your first period."

On the way Bradford thought about denial. It was amazing, really.

In the bad kids' chair sat a middle-aged Irishman in a good gray suit and tie. He looked like a bricklayer dressed up for church and reminded Bradford of the cops who had lived in the neighborhood when he was a kid, gruff men who had scolded him for putting pennies on the streetcar tracks, riding his coaster in the street, or setting grass fires on Corona Heights. They had never reported his offenses to his parents, and the memory of their indulgence now made Bradford feel especially guilty.

The man got up, introduced himself, sat down again. Bradford looked about, but the only chair was his old one, now Jesse's, behind the desk. Feeling sad, he took it.

"What can I do for you?"

The cop gave him a long look.

"You know Mr. John Rohrer?"

"Sure."

"Night before last he got beat up pretty bad."

"Really?"

"Mr. Rohrer and some of his friends think people here might have been involved. Whaddya think?"

"I doubt it."

"Mr. Bradford, were you one of the guys that did it?"

"I was not."

"Do ya know who did?"

"I do not."

"Mr. Rohrer thinks he's number one on your shit list. That right?"

"Close to the top."

The cop nodded.

Bradford told him about Rohrer's speech to the Board, and the cop nodded.

"Is he accusing me?"

The cop shook his head.

"Tell me who might have been mad enough to do it."

Bradford had been sitting on this pitch. He lined it back through the box.

"I have no idea."

"You just said—"

"—that people are pissed at him So what? We're not the Mafia here."

"Did you ever hear anyone threaten to harm Mr. Rohrer?"

"No."

"Tell me 'bout the people who were pissed. Who were they, wha'd they say."

Bradford sighed. "I won't implicate people for expressing their feelings."

The cop studied him. "You used to play football, huh?"

Another fan, thought Bradford. "Right."

"All-City."

"In my last year."

"You're pretty tough even now, I'll bet."

"I wouldn't say so."

"Mr. Rohrer said one of the guys was big. Could you tell me where you were on Saturday night between . . . say eight and midnight."

"Home."

"Wife with you?"

"I don't have one of those."

"Anybody else."

"I was alone. Listen. This is horseshit. If he knows one of them was pretty big, he also knows I wasn't the guy."

The cop finished writing in his notebook. Then, with some difficulty, he crammed it into his side pocket. He rose and stood gazing at Bradford, as if expecting something more.

Then he said, "The guys wore ski masks."

At noon Bradford went to the lunch room to hear the scuttlebutt on Rohrer, but nobody had any details. That night, before and during his meal, Bradford got moderately drunk and found himself stuporously ambivalent about the day's events. He was glad the little shithead had finally gotten what was coming to him; also, the fact that he himself was apparently a suspect renewed the self-righteous sense of grievance he had lately been nursing. On the other hand, he was uneasy. It seemed not impossible that he might be arrested, tried, and found guilty of this crime which he had not committed. One way or another, he supposed, the gods would punish him for what he <u>had</u> done.

At eight the telephone rang. Briefly he sat still. Then answered.

"Hello?"

"Mickey?"

The voice, strangely hoarse, was Janie's.

"Hey, Girly. What's up?"

"Did you hear about John Rohrer?"

"Yeah. Listen—you don't sound so good."

"I may be coming down with something."

"You should take some time off."

"Mickey."

"Yes?"

"Who do you think did it?"

"Not me."

116

"I know you didn't. But I heard that—"

"—a cop talked to me."

"Yes."

"It hurt me to do it, but I had to confess that I was totally innocent."

"That's not really funny."

"Sooner or later most males get beat up. It's a rite of passage. And I need not remind you that Rohrer is a very provocative little fellow."

"His eyesocket was crushed. He may lose vision."

"That bad."

"Yes."

"How did you hear about it?"

"From Gordon."

"Okay. I still think you shouldn't waste any sympathy on him. He does not wish you well."

"That's beside the point."

Not wish you well. A phrase from the broadside. He was becoming one of the boys.

"No, it's not. If we don't ration libido, we run out."

"An interesting notion," said Janie. "But not one I care to discuss at the moment."

"Janie, you really sound terrible."

"Stop changing the subject. Do the police really suspect you?"

"Apparently. Listen. Did Gordon give you any details?"

"Just that it happened at an ATM in Noe Valley."

"He was robbed?"

"Yes."

"Then it wasn't political! He was mugged."

"Gordon says they think that might have been a . . . what do you call it? A red herring."

"Rohrer's idea, no doubt. Paranoia."

"You can't know that."

"Janie. Take some medicine and go to bed."

"I probably will."

"Do it."

He himself went to bed but lay awake, thinking about a crushed eyesocket. Boxing and playing football, he had had three concussions, a broken arm and ankle, none of which had bothered him much; but he had always been terrified of injury to his eyes or balls. At last he got up, went downstairs, and looked through his mother's old Medical Encyclopedia for information about eye injuries. He found nothing to comfort him. Then he made a large Martini; the process calmed him a bit.

By now The Red Herring Theory seemed entirely plausible. In the dark of the den he counted circumstances on his fingers. The killing of the dog. The broadside. The advent of Briscoe. The nasty voices at the Board meeting. The men who had hailed him in the parking lot. The telephone call from the cheerful woman. And now Rohrer. It was too much.

At three he tried again to sleep, without success. At four he got up and dressed. He got the car out of the garage, drove out Sixteenth toward Potrero. The odds were that Rohrer was in City and County.

Emergency was a chamber of greenish light. Bradford thought of sci fi movies, space ships, aliens. People seemed to have auras. The receptionist checked her computer and said that Rohrer had been moved upstairs. She and the security guard watched Bradford closely.

"Can I find out how he's doing?"

"You can't go up there. If I can find the night nurse, you could talk to her on the phone."

"That would be fine."

The woman had him sign a book. Again he invoked Jay Berwanger. She found the nurse, handed Bradford the receiver. Bradford made his inquiry.

"His injury is serious. His condition is stable."

"Is his sight impaired?"

"You'd have to talk to the doctor about that. Are you a relative?"

"No."

"Hold on a minute."

Bradford waited. He imagined her calling the police. The nurse came back. "Listen. His mother's here. She's coming down to see you."

"No. Never mind. I'll call later."

"She's on her way."

Bradford handed the receptionist the phone, turned on his heel, and walked out. When he reached the sidewalk, he started to run. Home in fifteen minutes, he unplugged his phone. He drank a double shot of bourbon, which did not seem to have the slightest effect. Then he went upstairs, lay down in his clothes, and waited for morning.

TWELVE

At nine o'clock Bradford stood at a long counter in room 400 of the Hall of Justice. When a tall female officer approached him, he said that he had come to confess to a hate crime.

"What exactly did you do?"

He told her.

The policewoman, an attractive brunette with a dutch bob, raised her eyebrows and nodded, as if he had scored debating points. She opened a gate in the counter and led him to a small office where he was to wait. Except for a table and several chairs, all of battered yellowed wood, the room was bare and had a faint locker-room smell. He signed a temporary waiver of his right to an attorney. When she left, Bradford knew from the sound of the closing door that he was locked in. A half hour later a swarthy detective in jeans, t-shirt, and loafers arrived to hear and record his statement.

Bradford was a bureaucrat in the clutches of bureaucrats, and he entertained himself by imagining the circumstances. The policewoman was no more than a receptionist; perhaps she had gotten herself into trouble on the street.

The detective was a jack-of-all-work, probably on overtime. Someone had called in sick, others were out on investigations. He had not yet seen the real cops. This analysis of the institution did not make waiting easier. Bradford was exhausted. When the detective left, he rested his head on his forearms, tried to sleep, couldn't. At last he sat up, looked about, and decided they really ought to have magazines and Muszak.

It occurred to him that his discomfort was a sign of things to come. At last he began to brood, to suspect that he was experiencing something more calculated than the ordinary slow motion of bureaucracy. Probably they did not believe he had told the whole story. Probably they were trying to wear him down. Then again, maybe not. Nearly everybody hated work and those who occasioned it. *Let him wait* was a universal expression of revenge.

At last two more detectives arrived to repeat the questions of the first and ask others as well. One was middle-aged, the other quite young, both well-dressed and otherwise nondescript. The younger wheezed and blew his nose repeatedly. He smelled of Mentholatum, and Bradford worried about catching whatever he had. The detectives seemed interested, even sympathetic, and Bradford felt entitled to this sort of attention. He was not, after all, their usual customer.

At last the elder said, "You're gonna have to talk to a couple more people, Mr. Bradford. We don't know exactly when they'll show up. You need to go to the bathroom or anything?"

The younger escorted Bradford to the john. When he was returned to the room, the elder asked if he wanted a cup of coffee. Bradford said yes and was brought a small cup of stale lukewarm brew. He waited three more hours, during which he was allowed another toilet run and given a ham sandwich and a Diet Pepsi. He thought about *a couple more people* and decided they'd probably be Feds.

He was right. Shortly after two o'clock a man and a woman arrived and identified themselves as Special Agents Dillingham and Kaufman of the FBI. Though Bradford thought he had prepared himself for this news, the famous acronym sent a shiver through him. After all, he had grown up watching G-Man dramas on the tube.

When Bradford had finished the story of his own act, Kaufman asked him for all he knew about Briscoe and Wilson. He told them.

"Nothing else?" asked Dillingham. Bald and grave, he reminded Bradford of his internist.

"Nothing I can recall."

The agents looked at each other, then at him.

"We have one problem here, Mr. Bradford," said Kaufman. She was far and away the more interesting of the two, a tall black woman, broad-faced, a few years younger than Bradford. She was not pretty, but she had a wide, well-formed mouth and large, piercing dark eyes which made him uncomfortable. Voodoo Mama.

"Which is?"

"You say you blew the car because you were drunk and angry about your troubles. But you told one of the officers it was a hate-crime."

"Uh-huh."

"Well?"

"I don't know. I guess I wanted to be sure she took me seriously."

"Just blowing up a car isn't serious?"

Bradford could no longer meet the Voodoo stare. He was silent a moment.

"Look. You know Shapley? Seen him on the tube?"

Kaufman nodded slowly.

"Then you know he's an out-front, raging, obnoxious queen. I figured everybody would just assume I went after him for that reason."

"And now you say you didn't."

"No. Stereotypical gay behavior, in-your-face effeminacy, annoys me. But I don't hate gays."

"Really."

"Really."

Long silence.

"Mr. Bradford," said Kaufman at last, "who knows you're here right now?"

"Nobody."

"Did you tell anyone that you might turn yourself in?"

"No one."

What tangled webs, and all that. He had not come here to lie. He should have realized that he would have to, to keep Molly out of it.

The agents stood up.

"We'll get back to you, Mr. Bradford," said Kaufman.

In the bleak early morning Bradford had resolved to endure stoically, but now weariness got the better of him.

"Aren't you going to arrest me? I need to lie down."

At the door Kaufman looked back. Despite her loosely tailored dark slacks, Bradford noted what black folks call high ass. With one forefinger she pointed down.

"There's always the floor."

"Oh."

"Stay in sight of the little window."

Bradford lay down against the wall opposite the door, using his rolled-up jacket as a pillow. For a while he thought about his remarkable inconsistency, of which he had been absolutely unconscious until Kaufman seized upon it.

His honor as an educated man now required that he concede the possibility that he did in truth hate Shapley and

123

gays in general. But he resisted the idea as conclusion. It seemed to him a matter of definition. He probably hated Rohrer and Shabazz, but his feeling for Shapley and his ilk deserved a milder term.

Bradford fell asleep.

Dillingham and Kaufman returned an hour later. Bradford sat down across from them, rubbing his eyes.

"The night Mr. Rohrer was attacked, your colleague Wilson was working overtime."

"He was?"

"You didn't know that?"

Though Kaufman asked the questions Bradford sensed that she was the junior partner, under supervision. The FBI equivalent of a student teacher.

"No."

"Didn't you supervise the janitors?"

They've been busy, thought Bradford. "Not directly. Anyway, I' m not an AP anymore."

There was a long pause. Then Dillingham shifted in his chair, rested his forearms on the table. He clasped his hands and stared at Bradford. In his small blue eyes was not voodoo but something else just as disturbing, something still and threatening. Maybe just power. Yes. He was definitely the man with the fuzzy nuts.

"Here's what you're lookin' at, Mr. Bradford. Section 3838.1 of the State Code, pertaining to destruction of property, specifies six months to two years in the state penitentiary. But if the act is classified as a hate crime, that's a whole other ball game. The statute is brand new, and I don't have the text to hand. But you know it's serious. Also, it looks like you could have a problem with Section 6231 of the Federal Code for violating Mr. Shapley's civil rights."

Bradford nodded.

124

"So. We're talkin' two years at San Quentin or two years at Terminal Island. Maybe both. Maybe consecutively."

Bradford did not reply.

"But. We might be able to help you out."

"Really."

"Yeah."

"We have to ask you again, Mr. Bradford." Now Kaufman was the speaker. "This is real important. Does anybody—anybody—know you were coming here?"

"No."

"Any possibility you were followed?"

Bradford looked at her hands, long-fingered, veined, strong-looking. He imagined her using hand grips to prepare for the pistol range.

"I don't think so."

Again the agents looked at each other.

"Okay. Here's the deal," said Dillingham. "You stay on the outside, continue your relations with guys, and feed us what information you get. In return we do all we can to keep you from doing time. If you cooperate, if you're straight with us, we think we can come through for you."

"I'm not sure there's a whole lot more to get," said Bradford.

"You let us worry about that."

"If anybody questions them about Rohrer, they'll suspect I fingered them."

"Right now we don't plan to talk to them."

"You're not obliged to? Given what I've told you?"

"There's no other evidence," said Dillingham.

"You think Ones and Twos is a network? Bigger than they let on?"

"We don't know," said Kaufman. "That's one reason we want you out there."

"Okay. I'm game."

"You need to be sure," said Kaufman. "This could be dangerous."

"I'm sure."

"And there are conditions. You have to agree to a phone tap."

"No problem."

"We might have you wear a wire. You know what I'm talking about?"

"Yes."

"And you're willing?"

"Yes."

"Okay," said Dillingham. "Ms. Kaufman will be your case agent. When you have something for us, she'll be available twenty-four hours a day. You don't contact anybody else."

"Will I be under surveillance?"

"Sometimes. Not always."

At five-thirty that afternoon Bradford walked out of the Hall of Justice. Waiting for buses, he looked around for a tail, didn't see one. He caught the 42 to Market Street and the LRV to West Portal. He wanted to drink but did not care to run into people he knew. At the Philosopher's Club he ordered a boilermaker and savored his relief at being out. Fleeing Rohrer's mother, he had felt shame. Now it had faded. He did wish to make amends; but in the dim cave of the Philosopher's Club that desire was somewhat wispy. It belonged to the realm of the ideal.

Mainly, he wanted to save his own ass.

THIRTEEN

When Bradford got home he was slightly drunk and taking a mild, absurd pleasure in his new role. In the shower he spoke aloud, theatrically—"Special Agent Bradford!"

An hour later came the familiar hollowing cold in his solar plexus. He had told Kaufman and her partner nothing about Molly. In the dreary yellow room at the Hall of Justice he had of course known that the omission might undermine whatever credit his cooperation could obtain for him; but, feeling rather nobly protective, telling himself that the Feds might not care anyway, he had not dwelt upon the possibility. Now the truth seemed obvious: his concealment would cancel their obligation to lobby on his behalf; and, even if it did not, no judge who knew all the facts would be lenient.

He imagined himself on the telephone, telling the truth. "Ms. Kaufman, I forgot to say that I'm currently fucking a seventeen-year-old student."

Do that, and you'll be in the can by midnight.

The next morning before homeroom, Bradford found Molly in the lotus position before her locker, studying trig behind the waterfall of brassy hair. He squatted beside her and whispered.

"Meet me in the tutoring center at lunchtime. Bring your English book."

"Why?"

"I need to tutor you."

"Mr. Mysterious."

At noon, with her Norton Anthology open to "Sailing to Byzantium," they sat on plastic chairs angled into a carrel.

"Listen. I took your suggestion. Confessed my dastardly crime to the Feds."

Molly squeezed his forearm. "Good. What's next?"

"We shouldn't touch here."

"Okay." She let go.

"What's next is we have a problem. They want me to be an informer. To spy on these characters I told you about."

"Oooo. Radical."

"That means I'll be under surveillance sometimes. And I'll never know when. If we keep seeing each other, they're gonna find out about us."

"Oh."

"So we have to cool it till this is over."

"Mickey, I did some research. They can't <u>do</u> anything to you unless they actually catch us <u>doing</u> it. Because I'm certainly not going to testify against you in court."

"That's not the problem. I didn't tell them about you, and if they find out about us now, they'll decide I can't be trusted and toss me in the slam."

"Really?"

"Really. At the very least your parents would find out right away. And the Feds would probably question you. If they find a basis for prosecuting these characters—and

128

me—it's even possible you'd be called to testify. The whole business becomes public. You become notorious."

"Oooo."

"Oooo is right."

"God, Mickey. When you mess up, you do it big-time."

"Yeah. And one more thing."

"Shit. What?"

"If I bring these guys down, people in the Movement may look to get even. With me and anybody close to me, maybe."

Molly rolled her eyes. "God. If you knew all this might happen, why did you change your mind?"

"About confessing."

"Yes."

"I think they're going to kill somebody. If somebody doesn't stop them."

"Why do you think that?"

"You heard what happened to Mr. Rohrer?"

"They did that?"

"Probably. I can't be sure."

Briefly Molly put her head in her hands. Then looked up. "I can't believe this! Can't believe it!"

"There it is. But you're safe if we stay away from each other."

"For how long?"

"I don't know. Probably till you graduate."

"That's a long time."

"Not really."

"Will you still be interested?"

"Of course. Will you?"

She did not answer at once. "I think so. I don't know."

"That's a very intelligent, very adult response."

"Fuck intelligent." Now there were tears in her eyes. "Fuck adult."

129

"If you're going to cry, I'll have to leave, or everybody in the room will know what's going on. And I've just explained what that will mean."

"You are really cold-blooded!"

"Stop."

Abruptly Molly stood up, slid her backpack over her shoulder. She scooped up her text and binder, held them in the crook of one arm. Eyes wet, she gave him a glassy, satiric smile.

"Thanks <u>very</u> much for your help, Mr. Bradford!"

At one o'clock on the following Sunday, Briscoe called. Bradford could hear traffic in the background.

"How ya doin'?"

"Okay."

"Any problems after our little sortie?"

"No. How 'bout you?"

"None whatever. Listen. I'm goin' down to the gun show this afternoon. I thought you might like to come along. See some equipment. And people."

"Sure."

"Attaboy. Still in a fightin' mood?"

"Yeah. If we can be smart about it."

"Hey. We're the smartest. Be by in a half hour."

Bradford called Kaufman on a cell phone she had given him.

"Excellent. There's no time for a wire, but you'll be observed. Don't look around for them. He may watch you for that."

"You won't be there?"

"A black woman at a white boys' gun show? Be serious."

"Sorry."

Briscoe was right on time. And alone.

"Where's our little buddy?" asked Bradford, arranging his seat belt.

"I didn't ask him."

"Appreciate that."

"What's he got against you?"

"Ask him."

"Might have to."

"Fine with me."

"No offense. We just have to be careful."

Silence.

"You know, I really admire what you did."

"What, exactly?"

"How you called and raised. That night."

Bradford did not reply.

"'course you were sorta pie-eyed."

"Sorta."

"Would you be game for something bigger?"

"Probably."

"You'd have to be sober."

"I can do that."

"Okay. Listen. Do you really shoot? I mean, could you hit something besides a gas tank four feet away?"

"Not without practice. My Dad taught me to fire a pistol, but it's been years."

"Practice is no problem. And I can coach you a little."

"Okay."

"I could even recommend some weapons."

Bradford shrugged.

As they passed South City, Briscoe pointed out a low, flat-roofed building in a small industrial park just beyond the freeway.

"That's Hot Shot. Closest gun range to the city. We could go there."

"Who am I gonna shoot, by the way?"

Briscoe laughed. "Let's not get ahead of the game."

"Okay. But another little question, Boss."

"Go ahead."

"You've heard of my colleague, Mr. Rohrer."

"Yeah. He walked into something, didn't he?"

"I thought maybe he walked into you and our little pal."

As Briscoe laughed, Bradford turned his head to look, but there was no reading him.

"No. He didn't."

"Since you guys have a special interest in Hamilton, it entered my mind."

"Rohrer's nobody. I wouldn't waste my energy on him."

"No? I heard he's Alomar's buddy."

"Huh. Well, maybe I'm wrong."

"The thing is, Harley, if we're gonna work together, I'd like to know what's goin' on."

"You will. You have. Right now it's you, me, and Wynnie against the bad guys. Down the road there could be one or two others."

"Threes and Fours. The rules are changing."

"Gotta be flexible, Buddy. You're new in the movement, and ya gotta have a little trust."

"What do you do for a living?"

"Drive a truck. Long hauls."

"Uh-huh."

"Anything I know about you, you can know about me. That's another rule."

"All right."

After a pause Briscoe said, "But I'll tell you one more little thing. Just to show I trust you."

"What's that?"

"I smoked the nigger's mutt."

"No shit. I was sure it was Wilson."

"No. He'd'a been an obvious suspect. So he went to visit his sister in Bakersfield that weekend."

"And you used his keys."

132

"Right."

"And fucked up my life thoroughly."

"I couldna known that would happen."

"The Law of Unintended Consequences."

"Yeah. And that's partly why I wanted you to join up with us. To give you a chance to get even."

"With you or them?"

Briscoe laughed.

The gun show was in the main hall of a small suburban convention center. Hundreds of men browsed at thirty or forty stalls. The big gun manufacturers had set up mobile stores with cabinets and cases of polished wood and glass. In slacks, blazers, and name tags their salesmen smelled of barber shops and contrasted with the small gun dealers, scruffy characters in jeans and old t-shirts, outlandish beards or mustaches. They displayed their wares on ply-wood-and-sawhorse tables which sagged in the middle from the weight of weapons, ammunition, and surveillance equipment. Bradford laughed to see side-by-side booths established by dating and matrimonial bureaus.

His amusement seemed to offend Briscoe. "Gun people are loners," he said. "They need help meeting women."

Bradford stopped to look at books. *200 Quick and Easy Means of Revenge, Navy SEAL Combat Manual, Clear Your Record and Own a Gun, Just Say No to Drug Tests: How to beat the Whiz Quiz, Knife Fighting, Screw the Bitch: Divorce Tactics for Men.*

But Briscoc took his arm. "Come on. Want you to meet somebody."

They approached a table holding scoped rifles. Behind it stood a small man in fatigues and aviator shades.

"Mr. Briscoe!" The small man grinned. His teeth were brilliant, white, perfect. He had a short military haircut.

"Gunny: friend of mine, Mick Bradford."

Gunny removed his shades. He had small features and bright blue eyes which reminded Bradford of Wilson's, except that these bespoke calm and intelligence. Furthermore, Gunny was unacceptably handsome. No, thought Bradford. He was beautiful.

"Gunny knows more about scopes than any man in the world. Not just America. The world."

Gunny bowed slightly. "You a recruit, Mr. Bradford?"

"I guess."

"Can't guess. Gotta be sure."

"Okay."

Gunny and Briscoe discussed some items in stock. To Bradford their remarks were incomprehensible.

When they moved on, Bradford said, "If I were that guy, I wouldn't waste my time at gun shows."

"Whaddya mean?"

"I'd be out getting babes. A new one every day."

Briscoe laughed. "I think he does okay in that department. But he's also a man of discipline."

"Too bad."

"So that's your weakness."

"Probably."

"Would you rape a woman?"

To judge by Briscoe's expression, he might have asked about the weather.

"I don't think so. I like my women happy. Why do you ask?"

"I need to know your interests. Rape is a weapon. Gangbang the woman of one enemy, and you scare the living shit out of a hundred more."

"Really."

"Look at Haiti, Guatemala. Has to be done on the right scale, though. In Bosnia it got out of control. Got too much press."

Briscoe introduced Big Bob, another dealer, and to Bradford these two explained the virtues of the Accu-Tek HC38SS stainless steel autoloader. Bradford did his best to simulate interest and admiration. When they moved on, Briscoe said that Big Bob had been a mercenary in Africa and Indonesia.

"I can get you an excellent deal on that pistol."

"From Big Bob?"

"Or somebody else."

They stopped at another table where a young man solicited signatures for a state ballot proposition which would enable retired police officers and military men to carry concealed weapons. The young man had thick and shiny black hair, a ruddy complexion muted by close-shaven black bristles. Bradford thought of fire glowing under ashes and soot. The young man observed Bradford steadily. His raised eyebrows and the darkness under his eyes, along with round eyeglass frames, irises, and pupils, made concentric circles and suggested targets. Under the young man's stare it occurred to Bradford that he had been brought here for inspection. He and Briscoe went on to a stall displaying electronic eavesdropping equipment, and on the way Bradford looked back at the men he had met. Big Bob and Target-Eyes were busy with potential customers, but Gunny appeared to return his gaze. Because of the shades Bradford couldn't be sure.

On the way back to the city Briscoe said, "If you decide you want the pistol, give me a call."

"Okay."

Neither spoke again until Briscoe stopped in front of the house on States Street.

"I'm thinkin' about some real serious simultaneous actions. You, me, Wynnie, maybe one other guy. How does that sound?"

Bradford shrugged. "Okay."

Briscoe's next sentence came slowly, as if he were reciting a maxim from a book. "The actions will be chosen for their high probability of successful escape."

"Call me when you know more."

"Right."

"But you better think some about Wilson, Harley. He's outta control."

Briscoe laughed. "Don't worry. The night you blew the car, you took him by surprise."

"I've seen him lose it in other situations."

"When you and him had that fight?"

"Among others."

"Wouldn't you lose it if somebody busted your nose?"

"Not the way he did."

Briscoe grew serious. "Give the kid a break."

Bradford did not reply.

"With limited objectives, and under medication," said Briscoe, in his earnest recitation manner, "he's reliable."

"Medication?"

"Relax. When the time comes, I'll tell you about it."

"Jesus."

"Look. I know you've already done more than you've seen us do. But when the time comes, I'll make you a believer."

Bradford opened the car door. "Get the gun for me."

Briscoe laughed.

"You're somethin' else. Spooked one minute, rarin' to go the next."

"You need money up front?"

"Later."

"All right."

In the house, all Bradford could get on the cellphone was static. The next day he walked to McDonald's at Haight and Stanyan for lunch. On the way back he stopped in at a bar called the Aub Zam Zam, which was empty except for the owner, a famous eccentric named Bruno. Bradford dialed Kaufman's number. As he waited for her to pick up, the swinging door to his right was pushed open, but no one entered.

"A worthwhile afternoon," Kaufman told him. "Duly observed and recorded."

"Do you know those guys?"

"Some of them."

"Are they important?"

"Too soon to tell."

"Any idea what Briscoe has in mind?"

"Not a clue. You just keep us posted."

"I have a feeling they were looking me over."

"Probably."

"Why do I feel you're not telling me everything?"

"I tell you everything you need to know."

"Like Briscoe."

"We have a deal. You do something for us, we do something for you."

Walking back to school, Bradford worried about the swinging door. He decided that he had real potential as a paranoid.

FOURTEEN

Albert wore a <u>Beat Gal</u> button, a blue tee-shirt and white pants with fading food stains. Blue and white were the school colors. Since Albert did not seem at all the sort who would be a messy eater, Bradford assumed that somebody in the family worked at a restaurant.

They worked on dangling participles, four of which were to be found in Albert's most recent draft. On scratch paper Bradford wrote out two correct constructions as <u>Clair de Lune</u> tinkled and sighed in the background.

> Having broken the law, Mr. Mick was terrified.
>
> Mr. Mick, burdened by monstrous guilt, confessed.

"Okay. These phrases, which are built around verb forms, give information about Mr. Mick. So that my reader will know I'm talking about him and nobody else, I put the phrase either before or after his name. Now--look at what you wrote."

Bradford pointed to the boy's sentence.

Having come recently from China, life is
difficult on America.

"Your phrase doesn't quite work. Why not?"
Albert stared at the paper. He shook his head. On which
his hair, once again, was short and spikey.
"Who came from China? For whom is life difficult?"
"Me."
"But you're not in the sentence. So how do I know who
you're talking about?"
While Albert considered, Bradford glared at two boys
who had begun a game of blackjack at the next table. They
put their cards away, and Albert wrote "for me" at the end
of his sentence.
"Okay. You're getting the idea, but there's still a little
problem. In English, participial phrases don't usually mod-
ify objective case pronouns."
Bradford was afraid the kid would ask why, but he did
not. Albert appeared to be in physical pain. Bradford
thought he smelled soy sauce.
"Okay, okay—I'm getting too far ahead of the game,
grammatically. Try this. Rewrite the sentence and try to
make it like my examples."
Albert could not. At last Bradford revised for him.
"Okay. Our time's run out There are three more errors
just like this one and some other mistakes besides. Look for
them, try to correct them."
"You show where?"
Bradford sighed. He found two more danglers and un-
derscored them. "All right. But there's one more, and I
want you to find it yourself."
"Is hard."

"Yes. But if I correct all the errors, then you don't learn anything."

The kid looked miserable. Bradford couldn't bear it. He pointed to the <u>Beat Gal</u> button.

"You goin' to the game?"

"Yes."

"You understand football?"

Albert grinned, shook his head.

"What don't you understand?"

"Why Ham'ton never make touchdown. Always let other team try."

Bradford pointed out that Hamilton had fewer boys than other schools; that Hamilton kids had less time for sports than kids in other schools; and that Hamilton's mostly Chinese-American players were, on average, smaller than the players of others schools.

"But they don' <u>try!</u>"

Bradford laughed. "They <u>do</u>! Why do you think they don't?"

"Always kick ball to other team!"

"Not because they want to!" Bradford explained about first downs.

"Oh. <u>Oh</u>!"

"Enjoy the game."

As Bradford entered Janie's classroom through the back door, she was still alone, writing an assignment on the blackboard. Her lines were precisely horizontal, Spencerian and flawless. After taking a seat, silently, he diverted himself by trying to want her. He did not succeed, though he liked her as well as anyone he had every known.

It seemed to him that she had never been a young woman. On her second day at Hamilton she had come into his room to borrow chalk. "You bet, Sweetie," he had replied, never doubting that she was a student and probably a sophomore at that. Just a few years later, or so it seemed to him, she had become not middle-aged but <u>mature</u>. He could not remember when rills of gray had appeared in her soft blonde hair, when her skin had dried and a certain slackness had come into her soft face. But age had nothing to do with it, really—he had lusted after grandmothers. The problem was that morally and intellectually she was simply out of his league.

So he abandoned the effort and passed into a spell of mild nostalgia. Twenty years ago he himself had studied English in this classroom, which still had varnished oak wainscoting and four large, opaque, yellowish light globes, each set in the exact center of one quadrant of the ceiling. In her starched white blouse, gray skirt, and black pumps Janie might have been a teacher of that time. Outside it rained softly.

By three-forty-five the room was noisy with cordial talk, and Bradford surveyed the cast, doubting, as usual, that much would come of the meeting to follow. Janie and Joe, and Janie's pal, Lucille. Olaf Renstad, Santa-Claus-looking in his white beard and steel-rimmed glasses. Dapper Dennis Byrne, who along with Olaf had once led a radical faction of the AFT and whom the years had transformed into a wiseguy and womanizer. Aaron Ross, the faculty innocent. Lulu Bascombe, the faculty dingbat. Cal Hynes, for whom everything was old news. Rohrer, his head and eye bandaged. In recovery, he came to work only two or three times a week; but Bradford, who avoided him, had had no doubt that he would make this meeting. Most of the rest, almost a two-thirds majority, were women, teachers and parents whom Bradford viewed as inclined to caution and general niceness. Thirty adults, confined to and somehow infantilized by student desks—was that, Bradford wondered, why such meetings always felt futile?

At last the Colonel rose and went to Janie's podium. His mere presence quieted the room.

"The meeting will come to order. We have committee reports, I believe. Mrs. Ogawa?"

"Yes." She turned slightly, so that she could see those behind her. "We met with the Superintendent in his office last Thursday."

"Could you speak louder?"

Bradford scowled at Lulu, who had no manners.

"Yes. I'm sorry. We made our case to him. He thanked us and said he would think carefully about what we said. But he was completely non-committal."

"Which means that he's already made up his mind," said Lulu, as if Mrs. O. were incapable of reaching any conclusion on her own. Bradford had known Lulu since the sixth grade at McKinley Elementary School, where he had wished that she were a boy so that he could beat her up. In the ensuing years this desire had never left him.

"I don't think we should assume that," said Janie.

"Absolutely not!" said Aaron.

"Alumni Relations," said the Colonel, nodding to Gwen Chan.

"There have been fifteen or twenty phone calls, mostly by our retired people. They all say the response has been positive."

"Yeah, but look--what does that mean, exactly?" asked Dennis. "Any big shots committed to putting the screws on Alomar?"

"I believe some will go all out," said the Colonel, who was proud of his influential former students. "Jack Spelling at the Bank of America. Sam Crossley at the Chronicle."

"Can that kind of pressure work?" asked Bradford. "The town has changed so much."

The Colonel nodded. "That is a problem."

142

"Well, then," said Olaf. "How 'bout a little Direct Action?"

Silence. Some people looked embarrassed; others weary or resigned.

"I'm not suggesting we all hit the streets. Just those who have a taste for it."

"What do you have in mind, Oly?" asked Bradford. "Specifically."

"For openers, let's sit in at Alomar's office."

Another silence. At last Dennis Byrne said, "If, in its wisdom, this body determines that a sit-in is desirable, I shall put this aging body on the line."

Laughter.

"Who else?" asked Olaf.

"Like I said last time, I think Alomar's blowin' smoke," said Cal Hynes. "He hasn't got the cojones to close this place. But I'll do whatever my union brothers and sisters decide to do. Always have, always will."

"Kamikaze Cal," said Dennis.

Olaf turned to look at Bradford. "How 'bout you, Mick?"

Bradford nodded.

"Okay. That's four right here. And I know at least five others who will, teachers and alumni. And I'll bet we'll get kids as well. Ten or twelve people is plenty."

"We can't encourage the kids to do that," said somebody.

"We don't have to say a word," said Olaf. "Some will show up. Count on it."

"We also discussed an informational picket line at the next Board meeting," said Janie. "Maybe we ought to try that first."

"The Board'll have made up its mind by then," said Olaf.

"Yes," said Dennis.

"Joe. What do you think?" asked Gwen.

Leaning on the podium, the Colonel put the tips of his long fingers together. Then his gaze swept over those assembled. "You know that I regard 'Direct Action,' in its current sense, as the tactic of spoiled and pusillanimous children. I will of course picket. If you like, I'll make another speech to the Board. I'll call alumni, if somebody can get me a list of names and numbers. But at this point I am not sanguine."

"Pew-sa-what?" said Lulu.

Laughter.

"How about a bayonet charge, Joe?" said Dennis. "You could lead."

The Colonel looked at his pressing fingertips. He was blushing, so faintly that in all likelihood Bradford was the only one to notice. He had seen Joe Hensley blush just once before, twenty years earlier, and seconds afterward the Colonel had pitched an adolescent mocker bodily from the classroom. But now all he said was, "Tain't funny, McGee."

"How about some kind of public forum?" said Gwen. "We get people together from the various communities— say, in the aud on a Saturday—and see if we can work out our differences."

"That would have been a good idea last year or the year before," said Rohrer. "But now the only way you can possibly save this school is to change it—and fast. Though it may be too late."

Another silence. People looked at Rohrer. Bradford was now sorry the guy had been hurt, but he did not like him any better.

"Change it how?" asked the Colonel softly, as if mindful of Rohrer's weakened state.

"The main thing is to put in place a real affirmative action program."

"We have one," said Hynes.

"Tokenism. Twenty-five kids a year, not even three percent of the entering class. Nobody's impressed with that."

"Who's nobody?" asked the Colonel.

"I beg your pardon?"

"Who shares your view, besides the Superintendent and some activists?"

"Plenty of people."

"How do you know that?"

"I'm out there in the community. I talk to people every day."

"Anecdotal evidence."

"I think it's something to consider," said Gwen Chan. "And I say so knowing that more affirmative action would mean fewer kids from my own community. Suppose we suggest doubling the current number."

"Not enough," said Rohrer.

"The program we already have," said Bradford, "doesn't work."

Again, silence.

"Go on, Mickey," said the Colonel.

"By the beginning of the senior year, roughly forty percent of the affirmative action kids have transferred to other schools. Those who remain graduate with an average GPA of 2.3 and almost never meet the regular admissions criteria of four-year colleges."

"But they do go on to college," said Rohrer.

"That's not the point. Our job here is to prepare kids to meet regular admissions criteria and do regular, not remedial, university work; but we can't do that for the affirmative action kids because they're already too far behind when they get here. Anyway, they don't really need us. For community college, all they have to have is a 2.0. To get into State or Berkeley on affirmative action criteria, all they need is the approval of some committee of university ding-bats. They're much better off in comprehensive schools."

"How do you know all this, Mickey?" asked Lucille.

"You will recall that I was once a lordly administrator. I compiled the data from '91 to '94."

"Who else has seen it?" asked Rohrer. "I haven't."

"I don't know why you haven't seen it. Most people don't see it because the powers that be don't want them to see it."

"You were sworn to silence?" asked Aaron.

"More or less. But now I'm a disgruntled former administrator and to hell with 'em."

Laughter.

"But Mick," said Dennis, "to save the bloody school, wouldn't you agree to doubling the current number? Pragmatic fellow that you are?"

"Oh hell yes. But as Mr. Rohrer observes, at this point it's probably not enough."

"I move that we recommend to the Superintendent," began Janie, "that instead of closing the school he double the number of affirmative action students and establish a separate tutoring center for them."

"Jesus, Janie," said Cal. "Where do we get the staff for that?"

"Squeeze it out of the Central Office," said Gwen.

"Oh sure!"

"We can make it work somehow. I second the motion."

"Further discussion?" asked the Colonel.

No one spoke.

"All in favor?"

The *ayes* were wearily unanimous.

"Before we go," said Olaf. "Just so I can face Marie at dinner."

Laughter. In the sixties Olaf's wife had gone to jail in Mississippi.

146

"I move that this body support a sit-in by volunteers at the Supe's office."

"Second," said Cal.

The motion lost, with only Olaf, Dennis, Cal, and Bradford voting for it.

Afterward, on the way down the hall, Cal whispered to Bradford. "Buncha pussies. Literally and figuratively."

Bradford caught up with the Colonel in the stairwell.

"So. What do you think?"

"I think the end is coming."

"That bad."

"Yes. And at the moment I do not care to discuss the matter further. But I have a question for you."

"Which is?"

"Do you know the meaning of the word *pusillanimous*?"

"I think so."

"Do you think the rest of them do?"

Jesus, thought Bradford. His feelings are hurt. "I dunno. Janie would, of course."

"Of course."

In the foyer they stopped. The Colonel stood straight, looked over Bradford's head as if in high and private rumination.

"I felt as if I were talking to the children."

"Everybody was tired."

"No doubt. See you tomorrow."

Bradford returned to his classroom, straightened up his desk, and packed his briefcase with student essays. Lately he had been taking home work on weeknights, just in case he could persuade himself he was entitled to a day of sick leave to catch up.

The building was cold, silent, forlorn. Bradford still had an AP's habits, making slight detours on the way out to be sure that important doors were locked; but he would not

147

have gone as far as the gym had he not heard the thumping of a single basketball, which gave him a hunch.

From the open door he watched her move in a semicircle about one basket, practicing short fade-away jumpers. The brassy hair flew like a cloud as she darted after the ball, and he thought of dancers in a coffee table book he had at home. In the yellowish, grainy light her baggy pink shorts were like a tu-tu.

"Christ, Girl. Don't you have a home?"

In a graceful, arcing leap Molly picked off a rebound, landed, then pivoted to face him, holding the ball close. He was just a few feet away when it came at him and stung his hands, which he had raised just in time. Suddenly tongue-tied, he veered away from her, to the right baseline. Then he went up, took a shot. The ball ticked the rim, fell into her hands.

"Lame," she said.

"I'm not warmed up."

"Would it make a difference?"

"Maybe. Where is everybody?"

She dribbled the ball, thump, thump, thump. "No practice. Coach had a root canal."

"You're still pissed."

"Yes." In the vast space their words echoed. Actors, rehearsing in an empty theater.

"We have to do what I said."

"Then what are you doing here now?"

"They can't watch me here." Bradford felt that was true. But didn't know, really.

Again the ball flew at him, and again he got his hands up just in time.

"Play me some hunch," she said.

Bradford thought about it. "Okay."

"Take it out."

"I need to stretch a little first."

He went to the wall, placed his hands against it, leaned, stretched out his achilles'.

She watched for a bit and then said, "It must be awful to get old."

"Yeah? We'll see."

When he had finished he took four practice shots. Two were air balls. She caught the last one, returned it on a crisp bounce.

"Take it out."

"Oh, no. Ladies first."

She gave him a look, then dribbled out beyond the key. Turning, she came toward him. At the foul line she faked right, changed hands, drove left and went by him for a lay-up. She got the ball coming down and zipped it to him, grinning. In the coarse yellow light her coloring was like rouge.

"I could give you points," she said.

"Just wait."

Bradford took the ball out. He went left, but she was with him step for step. He reversed direction, drove into the lane, tried a hook. It banked, hit the front rim, wouldn't quite drop. Molly swept away the rebound, dribbled a few steps, fired a turn-around jumper. Swish.

Watching college teams on the tube, Bradford had of course realized that he could never stay with the best female players, the Millers, the Starbirds, the Azzis. Among true basketball players he had always been raw hamburger, his short career having peaked in the ninth grade. But Molly was *a high school girl*.

On his next possession he tried driving on her, but again she was too quick. He dribbled back out, put up a jumper, missed. She got the rebound, tried a hook, also missed. As the ball caromed high off the rim, he drifted under it, but Molly was beside him as it came down. They went up together, bumped in mid-air. His weight moved her aside,

149

but she had gone higher and her long, slim hand tipped the ball away. She followed it right, had it before he could even start toward her. She turned, gunned, buried it.

When she had retrieved the ball and flipped it to him, he just held it, looking at her.

"You were right."

"What?"

"It's awful to get old."

Her expression softened, ever so slightly. "Come on! You're not even breathing hard."

"It's not my wind. I'm slow. And I can't get off the floor."

"Too many sticky buns."

From beyond the key he took an old-fashioned one-hand set shot and, to his surprise, drained it. For a time he stayed close, hitting a baseline jumper, then putting back a rebound after screening her out. The ball and their foot-steps made intermittent thunder. The dolly hair flew and swept, teasing his face when he guarded closely.

It was 14-8 when he drove for a layup and they collided. Molly went sprawling.

He held out a hand. When he pulled her up, she was close.

"That a charge, you think?"

"Yes!"

He understood that he could not compete unless he used his weight, pushed her around on the inside. In the old days that had been his forte, banging the boards, getting easy points off rebounds in heavy traffic. His junior high coach had called him "garbageman," after a well-known USF forward with comparable gifts.

He stayed outside and missed four long jumpers. She finished him off.

"You quit on me," she said.

"I was never in it."

They sat down on wrestling mats stacked in a corner. Bradford looked at his watch.

"Jesus. It's almost six. You have your dad's car?"

"No."

He was about to say he would drive her home, then remembered that he couldn't. When he turned toward her, she was already looking at him. Eyes are not so much the windows of the soul, he thought. More like traffic signals, and hers had changed. He kissed her. They did their familiar thing, lips darting, touching noses, cheeks, brows. Mouths locked, tongues fought. When his hand moved under her waistband, she caught his wrist.

"Turn out the lights, Doofus!"

Bradford crossed the gym and closed the door. Then he went to the metal box on the wall. Before hitting the switches he looked back at her. She was a brown study, her hands clasped in her lap, her face turned way from him.

The place went pitch dark. Bradford headed for the mats. But when he did not reach them after twenty-odd steps, he raised his hand and struck his knuckles on the wall he had nearly walked into. They stung; made him angry.

"Where are you?"

Silence.

He moved left, feeling the wall. His shin and knee hit the piled mats and he nearly fell.

"Damn. Don't play games!" He put his hands on the mats and began to feel his way along.

She grabbed his shirt and pulled him forward onto the mats. Then she was atop him, holding him in a bear hug, whispering in his ear.

"You are old. You can't play basketball. You can't even see!"

He reached back, found her waistband, then groped her crotch.

"Wet little pussy."

151

"Dry little cock!"

It took all his strength to break her grip and roll her over. When he got to his knees and again fumbled for the waistband, she was clutching it with both hands.

"No! I want foreplay!"

"No foreplay. Brutal violation."

"Foreplay!" The word seemed to make her hysterical.

He tickled her to make her let go, then held her till she stopped laughing.

It was seven o'clock before they finished. He waited outside the locker room while she showered and dressed. For a time they embraced in hallway shadows, near a street door.

"Do most people do it that long?"

"I don't know. Maybe when they haven't done it for a while."

"Oh. Well, we hadn't, right?" She seemed reassured.

"Right."

"What's happening with those guys?'

"Nothing at the moment. Maybe something soon."

"Will it be over then?"

"Except for whatever happens in court."

"Are you in danger?"

"I don't think so."

"I've thought about it a lot. The whole business. I think I'm getting used to it."

"Uh-huh."

"Mickey: I'm hooked now. Can't do without you."

"You hardly know me."

"Yes I do."

"I'm still going to do the rest of it, though. College, I mean."

"Of course."

"Can I help you?"

"With what?"

"The stuff with those guys."

"No. You absolutely have to stay clear of it."

He made her leave by a side door, then decided he should stay until she was long gone. He climbed the stairs to the third floor. The lights were on, and at the far end of the hall Wynn Wilson was sweeping. The sight gave Bradford a shock. It should have occurred to him that the kid might be around—and possibly snooping. He couldn't have gotten into the gym without being heard, but he might have seen Bradford enter. Might have known that Molly was already there.

Bradford unlocked his room, turned on the lights, and spent a half hour bringing his attendance records up to date. He half-expected Wilson to appear in the doorway. Wilson who hated him and no doubt owned a gun. He could just walk in, start shooting.

But probably wouldn't. The odds were against it. Bradford figured they would hold.

FIFTEEN

At seven o'clock on a Saturday evening Bradford stood with Cheryl Kaufman in a vacant office suite south of Market. Briscoe had invited him over for beer and talk, and she was fitting him with a wire. Inhaling her light cologne, he felt her breath on his naked shoulder as she adjusted the harness. He had an erection. It seemed to him that a young man and a young woman, alone in a secret place, should inevitably and naturally fuck, regardless of whatever else they had to do.

She took his hand, guided it to the tiny, flat recorder suspended under his arm.

"Feel the switch?"

"Uh-huh."

"Push it hard, hear it click, and the little sucker will run for three hours."

"Okay."

"Put on your undershirt."

He did. When the cloth had passed his eyes, she had taken a full step backward and was scowling.

She handed him the tiny microphone. "Bring it up under your shirt! Out the neck!"

He did. Reaching, bending from the waist, she clipped the microphone to the neckband of the undershirt.

"Sorry."

"I don't require your apology. Put on your shirt and get going."

The weather had turned cold enough for Bradford to see his breath. The engine of the old Buick had died once on the way to Kaufman and did so again before he reached Briscoe's place.

The house was a well-kept, one-story shingled place in the Excelsior. Among its boxy stucco neighbors, it seemed out of place and reminded Bradford of small towns. On the cupola of the porch was a red-and-white <u>For Sale</u> sign.

"Nice place."

"Damn right. But just try and sell it."

"Really? I thought the market was good."

"Not out here." Briscoe shut the door behind them. They passed through a living room which struck Bradford as oddly impersonal, like a display in a furniture store.

Briscoe seemed to read him. "My wife took a lotta stuff when she left."

"Uh-huh."

"Took the kid too."

"Sorry to hear that."

"Man's got no chance in divorce court."

As Briscoe led him down narrow steps, Bradford locked the switch of the recorder.

In the garage two ancient cars were bumper-to-bumper, Wilson's green Colt and a white Falcon Bradford had never seen before. Chemical smells, gasoline and something else, made him think of anesthesia. There was the yellowish, match-like flaring of naked bulbs. One, in a metal cage, lay atop the battery of the Colt. Wilson and Big Bob stood peering at the blackened engine. Big Bob looked up, nodded to Bradford. Wilson ignored him.

Briscoe removed the caged light, closed the hood and then the stairwell door.

"Leave 'er here tonight," he said to Wilson. "I'll do 'er tomorrow."

The men stood by as Briscoe washed his hands in a tub at the rear, beside a washer-dryer. Then he led them into a room adjacent to the garage. Hung on the door was a framed engraving of Jews crowded into a boxcar. There was something odd about it--something, that is, besides its being there in the first place. Bradford stopped to look.

"I did that last year," said Briscoe. "I still think it's funny."

Bradford saw the joke. Briscoe had darkened each face with pencil.

"My idea is, Hitler had the right idea but the wrong minority group."

"Uh-huh."

From a small coffee table Wilson and Briscoe retrieved cans of beer. The room smelled of it. They sat down in wicker basket chairs, Bradford on a small, puffy black sofa. He looked around as Briscoe got more beer from a small refrigerator. There was a black shag rug, a gun safe, and a portable TV playing softly on an old typewriter table. On the longest wall were two more framed images, group photographs of football teams. JV's and varsity, Bradford guessed.

"Myself, I've never had a problem with Jews," said Briscoe, handing Bradford a beer, then sitting beside him. "Okay--they're pushy and greedy, but what the hell. That's the American way. Whaddayou think, Bob?"

Big Bob hesitated, giving Wilson a cigarette, then lighting one himself.

"They ain't the main problem," he said at last, looking at Bradford, to whom his accent seemed generic country-western. "You heah all this stuff 'bout a Zionist Con-

156

spiracy. But shit—the country's too fucked up to be run by a conspiracy."

"That's what I think," said Bradford.

"Rohrer's a Jew, ain't he?" asked Wilson.

The reference seemed to come out of the blue. Bradford turned toward the kid; tried to look friendly.

"I believe he is, yeah."

Briscoe nudged him. "I forgot. You're a boilermaker man. Want a shot go with that?"

"Not tonight," said Bradford.

"Boilermaker," said Big Bob. "That's a man's drink."

"A drunk's drink," said Bradford.

"I'm still wondering," said Briscoe, "if you have a problem."

Bradford sipped his beer. "You decide."

Briscoe laughed. He looked at Big Bob, inclining his head toward Bradford. "One thing I like about him. Doesn't give a shit what anybody thinks."

Big Bob gazed at Bradford. In a gray t-shirt and blue jeans, he looked like a farmer cleaned up for town. He had a pink face and bifocals.

At last he said, "Good way tuh be."

Wilson had tuned out. He was watching TV.

"What's on, Wynnie?"

"Don't fuckin' call me that, Harley. I tol' you."

"Whoops. Forgot."

"Bullshit you forgot."

"Babes," said Briscoe.

"Miss U.S.A.. Check it out."

They watched the swimsuit parade.

At last Briscoe said, "Gang and bang 'em."

"Deck 'em and dick 'em," replied Wilson. "Flop 'em and hop 'em."

"Munch 'em and punch 'em."

Wilson looked at Briscoe. "What's that supposed to mean?"

"You eat their pussies and then you fuck 'em."

"Ah, man!"

"Your turn."

"Suck 'em and fuck 'em."

"That's not original," said Briscoe. "Everybody says that."

"Perverts," said Big Bob, looking at Bradford. "Down home they'd be humpin' sheep."

"Me and Wynnie make up rhymes about fuckin' women," said Briscoe. "But we're not very good at it."

"Uh-huh."

"You try."

Bradford thought for a moment. "Ground 'em and pound 'em."

"Not bad," said Briscoe.

"Whaddaya mean, 'Ground 'em'?" asked Wilson.

"He means put 'em on the ground, Dummy!"

"Stroke 'em and poke 'em."

"Hey!"

"Spank 'em and plank 'em. Mug 'em and plug 'em."

Briscoe whooped. Even Big Bob laughed..

"Dope 'em and grope 'em."

"See Wynnie, it takes an English teacher to do it right."

"Fuckin' psycho English teacher."

"Look who's talkin'," said Briscoe.

"Thump and hump. Whup and *schtup*."

"*Schtup*?"

"Means *fuck*," said Bradford. "It's Yiddish, I think."

"You wouldn't happen to be Jewish, would you?" asked Big Bob.

Bradford coughed several times. The smoke was getting to him. He thought about Kaufman listening to the tape, later. At last he shook his head.

158

"You could pass, though," said Briscoe. "Jews are known for high verbal intelligence."

"I thank you."

"Smoke bother you?"

"A little."

"Most people in the Movement smoke," said Briscoe. He studied Bradford, as if the fact might be defining. "I could open the door, but then we'd get the gas smell."

Bradford cleared his throat. "No problem."

"Hey!" Briscoe stood up, went to a small cabinet. "Since we're on the subject of puttin' ladies in their place, I got somethin' to show you guys."

He took out a video tape, changed the TV channel. Then he put the tape in the VCR and turned out the lights.

"Have a look. "

The tape began with the image of a plank floor. Then the camera swung wildly, up and down, back and forth. Trees from an open window, a wall with burlap hung on it, a woman's bare calf, the planks again. Then a sudden flash of unbearable sunlight, blue sky, masses of trees.

At last the camera focused on a small frame house. Sunlight glared on its facade, porch, peeling paint, and a small dirt yard in front.

Shouting figures filled the doorway, spilled onto the porch. Two were tall black men in white shirts and white trousers cut off at the knee. Each held one arm of a small, naked Caucasian woman. Her breasts were small and slack, but she was otherwise well-formed. As they hustled her down the steps two more men emerged from the house. One clutched a rumpled blanket to his chest. He spread it on the ground a few feet in front of the porch. Dust rose and swirled.

For the next half hour the men took turns with the woman, who appeared dazed. They would mount her, move slowly for a time, hump madly as they started to come.

Those waiting their turns capered in the dust and mugged for the camera or wagged their members at it. The camera kept jiggling, and Bradford became slightly seasick.

When the first man began his second turn, Wilson spoke hoarsely. "Shit! How'd he get it up again so fast?"

"Animals," said Bob.

The tape ended as one man draped the woman over the porch steps and sodomized her.

Bradford looked around. Big Bob looked sleepy. Wilson had an erection, and Bradford remembered himself with Kaufman.

"Where'd you get this?" asked Wilson.

"Contact of mine. He says the niggers are Inkatha guerrillas. The woman's supposed to be the wife of an Afrikaner they just killed. Whaddya think, Bob?"

"They're Africans," said Big Bob. "Tell ya that."

"Mickey?"

"Anybody can hire a whore to fuck on camera. In Africa or anywhere else."

"That's true," said Briscoe. "I wouldn't bet the farm that it's for real. But in my gut, I think it is."

"Me too," said Wilson, still hoarse.

"Even if she's a hooker, it's awful to watch," said Briscoe. "Sort of like the end of the world. I could burn those niggers alive, six inches of skin at a time, and never miss a wink of sleep."

"You take it too serious," said Big Bob.. "A douche and a bath, an' she's the same ol' girl again."

"Knew you'd say that."

"It's the truth."

"Imagine this, though," said Briscoe. "A small commando team takes over CBS News at six-forty-five on a Sunday night. Then they show this instead of *Sixty Minutes* "

Big Bob laughed.

"Guy I got it from thinks we can use it as a recruiting film. But I dunno. Look at ol' Winnie. He's rock-hard."

"I watch sex, I get it up. That's normal."

"This ain't sex," said Briscoe. "It's . . . I don't know what."

Big Bob had been looking at Wilson. He seemed to give everyone long looks. But now he turned to Briscoe.

"That cute little wife of yours," he said. "You real sure she didn't take some big buck back home with her?"

Bradford held his breath. Briscoe said nothing.

"Think about all them long days. Kid's in school an' she's all by her pretty little self in a neighborhood fulla blacksnake."

Bradford exhaled, slowly. He remembered reading that men in prison tormented each other in this way.

"It's a question we all ask ourselves," Briscoe said at last. "Women are weak vessels. But I don't think mine could."

"What would you do," asked Wilson, "if you found out she did?"

"I'd beat her bloody. Then I hope I'd be man enough to load my car with ordnance and go kill the particular nigger. Then maybe drive out to the Point and waste every other one I could find. Till the cops got me."

After a moment Bradford asked, "Harley. How come you do what you do?"

"What?"

Again Bradford coughed. Then he said, "Instead of putting on a sheet and burning crosses. Or marching in an SS uniform. Or playing war games in the boonies."

Big Bob threw back his head and laughed. Briscoe grinned. Bradford thought he might be blushing, but it was difficult to tell in the dim light.

"I've done all those things." He nodded toward Big Bob. "He knows. Spent half my life doin' 'em."

"And?"

"Now I know that only action matters."

No one replied.

"Remember how the Skinhead took out that Ethiopian in Portland? After that, every jungle bunny in the country knew it could happen to him. And every guy like us said, 'Hell, I can do that!'"

"Takin' out one nigger every six months," said Big Bob, "ain't gonna get it done."

"Any one thing could be the spark. The thing that sets it off. Like with the assassination of that Archduke."

"Like what?"

"Wynnie. You need to get yourself a little more education."

"Fuck you, Harley."

"What got you interested in Hamilton?" asked Bradford.

The question seemed to catch him off guard. He hesitated. "It's a great institution, and the mud people want to destroy it."

"Bullshit," said Wilson. "You said—"

"—Awright, Awright!" Briscoe held up his palm. "I was just gonna say. It's a personal matter, too. My kid got rejected there."

"Oh," said Bradford.

"She had sixty-two points. The cut-off for white kids was sixty-three."

Bradford nodded.

"Without fuckin' affirmative action, sixty-two woulda been enough, right?"

"Depends on how many others had the same score."

"But probably."

Bradford did not reply.

"Right?"

"Yeah."

"See, I always regretted not goin' there myself."

162

"Really."

"Yeah. That is, after I had sense enough to know it woulda been a good thing. At the time my grades weren't good enough. I was kind of a fuck-up."

"Uh-huh."

"But yours were."

"What?'

"Your grades."

"Oh. Barely."

"Anyway, my kid wasn't like me. She was a good student. She played the game, and the fuckers still wouldn't let her in."

"Shit, I wouldna gone even if I'd lived here," said Wilson. "Even if I'd had the marks. Too many brown-nosers and goody-goods."

"You're kinda . . . anti-intellectual, Wynnie."

"Fuck intellectual."

Big Bob broke in suddenly. "So. Hahley. Tell us what's on your mind."

"Is something on his mind?'"

"Yeah. Hah-ley ain't a big socializer."

Wilson laughed.

Briscoe sat up straight, as if Big Bob had called him to attention. There was a pause.

"I mentioned the possibility," he began, looking first at Wilson and then at Bradford, "of simultaneous actions."

Bradford nodded.

"The planning is almost finished."

No one spoke.

"Tonight I gotta ask you for a commitment. Make it and you're in all the way. Nobody backs out."

"What's it gonna be?" asked Wilson.

"The general picture is this: we fuck up some of Nigger Freddy's pals. And soon. The details come later."

Bradford coughed again. The smoke, the beer, the slow passing of his seasickness, left him oddly detached. His strongest feeling all evening had been his humiliation before Kaufman. Now he thought of boys in treehouses, with wooden swords.

"So. You commit now, or you get up, walk out, and never say a word about this to anybody, ever."

Silence.

"Wynn?"

"Fuck, yes. I tol' you I would."

"Mickey?"

Bradford nodded. "But I assume we're lookin' at serious jail time if we get caught. So I think you should take us into your confidence."

Briscoe gazed at him. "Can't do that yet. And you know why."

Bradford shrugged. Tried to look cranky. He raised his fist.

"Ones and Twos!"

"It's no joke, Mickey. You in or out?"

"In."

"You sure?"

"Yeah."

"All right. I should tell you—both of you--that Bob probably won't be part of this. He's here tonight mainly as an observer, an adviser. I can guarantee his silence."

"But I'll help out tomorrow."

"Right. That's the next thing." He got up, went to the cabinet, returned with a stack of paper from a lower shelf. He handed a sheet to each of the others.

"What I have in mind," he said, "is a little public information campaign."

Bradford read.

ATTENTION NIGGERS

BEEN THINKING ABOUT A LITTLE VACATION? BACK TO THE SOUTH TO VISIT YOUR APE RELATIVES AND PRACTICE SWINGING FROM TREE BRANCHES? <u>NOW IS THE TIME.</u> BECAUSE BIG TROUBLE IS COMING FOR THE GREASE BALLS AND JUNGLE BUNNIES OF THIS TOWN. BETTER MOVE YOUR BLACK BUTTS, BROS, AND SOON.

"Whaddya think, Mickey? As an English teacher?

"Uh." Bradford was mystified. He had read *BROS* as *BROZ*. Then he got it.

"Very alliterative."

"Is that what they call it?"

"Yeah."

"With these, we let 'em know something is coming. So that when it's done they know we can do whatever we want."

"Whadda we do with 'em?" asked Wilson.

"We post 'em in the heart of niggertown. At six tomorrow morning."

"Why not tonight?"

"The cops change shifts between six and seven, and nearly all the black-and-whites are at the station house."

"It'll be daylight," said Bradford.

"Gotta be <u>some</u> risk. We gotta . . . test our nerve."

"Which niggertown?"

"Whaddya mean?"

"Hunter's Point? The Western Addition?"

Briscoe looked at him. "What difference would it make?"

165

For the first time Bradford thought he heard suspicion. After a moment he said, "Whites are too conspicuous at the Point. And there are very few routes out of the area."

"Hey! Good logistical thinking." Briscoe pronounced the word with a hard g. "And you're right The target is the Fillmore."

"What do we do between now and six?" asked Bradford. "I'm getting sleepy."

"Smoke really bothering you."

"More than usual."

"Well, do what you want. I got three empty beds upstairs. Or go home and sleep if you want. I'll pick you up on route. Five-forty-five."

Briscoe brought out another round of beers. When Big Bob reached for his, Bradford noticed a zig-zag scar on his upper arm. They made small talk and watched the crowning of Miss U.S.A., during which Wilson contributed, "Tape 'em and rape 'em!" Briscoe and Bradford clapped.

At last Bradford stood up. "Gonna head out."

"One thing," said Briscoe.

"What's that?"

"No more booze, okay?"

"Aw. Your lack of confidence is disheartening."

"I need to see how you do without it."

From an Irish bar on Eighteenth Street Bradford called Kaufman.

"Got it all," she said. "And we'll be with you." She sounded sleepy. Bradford imagined the long limbs, the high ass, under nylon and warm covers. Lace decolletage.

"Sorry to wake you."

"You didn't."

"He didn't say much."

"No surprise."

"Sometimes I think they're not for real," said Bradford. For some reason he wanted to keep her on the line.

"Don't underestimate him. He's been around some nasty stuff. Just what part he's played, we don't know."

"You found out more?" Bradford listened closely for sounds of a companion. Heard none.

"Some. Not much."

"Anything I should know?" He was beginning to feel better. Kaufman no longer seemed angry, and he would have a boilermaker before going home.

"Nothing that would make a difference."

"What's the story on big Bob?"

"Possibly dangerous. Like the others."

"He seems to like me."

"I wouldn't buy into that."

When Bradford hung up, he had no erection. What he did have was a little crush.

Unobtainable women. They were everywhere.

Briscoe was right on time. Thin ice edged his windshield and rear window.

"Get some sleep?" he asked.

"Not enough. Next time, how about a little notice?"

"You gotta learn to operate under stressful conditions." Briscoe was *The Commandante* again, tense and full of himself. "Everything can't be perfect."

"Wilson with Bob?"

"Yeah."

"What's the story on Bob?"

"Mickey. You ask too many questions."

Bradford decided to push. "How come you took all that shit about your wife?"

Briscoe did not reply at once. "Bob is one of the Elders. He advises us. And tests us."

"This his idea?"

167

"No. That's not what I meant."

"What, then?"

"Damn, you love to talk. Look. When my wife left me, I swear I was gonna smoke 'er. I had my ordnance, see, and I was gonna catch up with her at the airport. Bob talked me out of it."

"How?"

"He said I was being a pussy."

"Oh."

"He said when you need one woman too much, your cock and balls shrivel up. She makes a woman out of you."

Bradford said nothing.

"I decided he was right. But now and then he puts me to the test. To see if I'm really cured."

"Are you?"

"Pretty much. I guess not entirely."

"Tell me about today."

"I drive, you put up the signs. There's a staple gun in back. Should go quick and easy. We're gonna skip every other block and make lots of turns, so we don't spend much time in any one area."

"Okay."

"By the way: for the major actions, it wouldn't hurt to brush up on the Vehicle Code. You'll want to be the most law-abiding driver ever was."

They fell silent. Bradford grew forlorn and oddly nostalgic. At this hour and in such weather he had once delivered newspapers. He had liked being outside and alone in the morning silence, getting a head start on everybody else. It had been a different town then.

After crossing Webster on Eddy, Briscoe slowed to a stop.

"Start here. Do two or three on each side, then meet me at the corner. Walk fast but don't run."

Bradford got out, took the staple gun and handbills from the back. He posted two on telephone poles, one on a wood fence. Then he crossed the street, hit two more poles and the garage door of an abandoned house. The cold made him want to run.

When he got back in the car, Briscoe grinned at him.

"Easy as pie, right? Nobody notices."

By the time they'd done ten blocks Bradford was breathing hard.

"Two more and we quit. I been watchin' the cross streets. Haven't seen one black-and-white."

Bradford nodded.

"How 'bout you?"

Bradford shook his head.

Briscoe looked at him intently.

"So I got it right."

"I guess you did."

Bradford was on the last block when it happened. He was stapling a handbill to a fence and heard footsteps. He looked left and saw an elderly black man with a dog on a leash. Bradford started; and later he would decide that only this guilty movement had caught the man's attention. He turned away, hurried up the street.

Midway down the block was a defunct store, its windows recently covered by clean plywood. Not even the graffiti artists had gotten to it yet. As Bradford stapled, the remaining handbills slipped from beneath his arm. He cursed, bent down. They lay flat, and his fingers slipped over their surfaces as he tried to pick them up. He had just gotten the last one when he felt the hand close on his arm.

He rose quickly, pulling away. But the hand was like iron.

"Man. Why you wanna do this?"

The voice was stern, but the words were not complaint or curse or challenge. They were a simple question.

169

"Let go. Please." Bradford tugged harder but the old man hung on. Bradford thought of his father.

"Why? What we done to you?"

Bradford bent from the waist, used the strength of his legs. For a moment the old man held on, stumbling with him toward the corner, but then he let go. Bradford ran to the car.

"Wha'd he do?" asked Briscoe.

"Get us outta here."

Turned sideways in the seat, Briscoe stared at the old man. "Look at him," he murmured. "Look at the black bastard."

"Go!"

Suddenly Briscoe made a u-turn, throwing Bradford against the door.

"What the fuck, Harley!"

The car bumped over the curb and they were hurtling down the narrow sidewalk. Bradford saw the side mirror strike a pole, disappear.

Thirty yards ahead the old man and his dog stood frozen.

"NO!"

The old man took two high, stiff comic steps toward some steps. He looked like a dancer in a minstrel show. Then he dove.

Briscoe whooped. Bradford turned and saw the old man sprawled on the steps. At the corner Briscoe slowed, let the car bump from curb to pavement, and turned left. Bradford looked each way down the first side street, waited for Kaufman and her people to converge on them.

It didn't happen. A minute later he and Briscoe were cruising out Divisadero in a pack of other cars.

"Okay, Mick?"

"Okay, _what_?"

"You believe I'm serious?"

Bradford shivered. It was as if Briscoe had overheard his talk with Kaufman.

"You made a mistake out there. The nigger got a look at you. The moment he took hold, you shoulda come up swingin'."

"He was an old man."

"He's a fuckin' subhuman ape nigger, but he could pick you out of a lineup. You shoulda busted his head."

They did not speak again until Briscoe made his right onto States.

"Don't take it personally. I'm givin' you constructive criticism."

When they stopped in front of the house, Bradford sat still for a long moment, gazing straight ahead. Then he turned to Briscoe.

"If I do better on the final, can I still get an A in the course?"

Briscoe laughed. He slapped Bradford on the shoulder.

SIXTEEN

Bradford stood behind his front door until he could no longer hear the car. Then he walked to Walgreen's on Castro, bought Sominex, and reported to Kaufman on the cellphone. He emphasized Briscoe's run at the old man.

"We didn't see it," she said. "We lost you half way through."

"Great."

"Had to keep back. There was no traffic to give cover. He made some turn we missed."

"Look. I am now a believer. He intends to kill people. Can't you get him off the street?"

"I'll look into it. Calm down and get some sleep."

Again Bradford did not want to let her go. Apropos of nothing he said, "Ol' Bob gives me the creeps."

"He should."

"Why?"

Kaufman sighed. "He spent sixty-seven months and thirteen days in Vietnam."

"Jesus Christ."

"He was one of the early advisers that Kennedy sent, and he just kept re-uping. We figure he's looking for a war to win. Or maybe just one to get killed in."

Bradford went home to bed, and the Sominex worked. He awoke at two in the afternoon and sat for a time on the edge of his bed, trying to decide if an antihistamine hangover compared with the genuine article. Then he showered, dressed, and left the house. He drove all the way out Divisadero and parked at the Marina Green.

The gods had suddenly suspended winter; it was a clear, perfect day, temperature in the sixties. Gazing north along the shoreline, one could have disbelieved in the automobile, assumed the bridge was for people and horses. Lately such days came only when things went badly, and Bradford took this as an omen. See what you've lost, it said. Maybe forever.

At the yacht harbor he found a public phone, from which he called Molly's house. Something he'd never done. "Oh, Hi!" she said, so cheerily that he knew she could not talk. "Listen—I'm in a rush. Can I call you tonight?"

"Sure. Talk to you later."

He hung up, certain she'd be angry. "Don't ever call me at home!" she had said. "There're extensions all over the house. Half the time all three of us pick up at once."

He walked toward the bridge, first along the shore, then on the path through the Presidio. There were hundreds of runners, nearly half of them women in nylon and spandex. They were splendid; and he was sure that not one had a problem with answering the phone when a lover called. He could have made a life of screwing such women and never gotten himself into trouble remotely like what he had now.

On Monday, the first day of Christmas vacation, there was a brief article in the *Chronicle* about the appearance of hate literature in the Western Addition. It spoke of a

173

"general threat to Latinos and African-Americans" and said the police had no clues. The next day, in a run-off, Freddy Lamar defeated the incumbent by two percentage points. The fact compounded Bradford's unease.

That night Kaufman called. She asked him to meet her for lunch the next day in the financial district.

"Dress up," she said. "Look like a business person."

Bradford owned one suit, gray with pin-stripes. For years he had worn it only to Open House and Graduation; it made him feel like a best man or a pallbearer. He took the LRV downtown from Castro Street in a crowd of Christmas shoppers. He had, insofar as possible, ignored Christmas for years, and he was unaccustomed to both public transportation and people who had nothing to do with public schools. Leaving the train, he felt slightly dazed, as if he had just arrived in a non-English-speaking country. Not for the first time he wondered how he had become the person he was.

He met her at a restaurant called Splendido in the Embaracadero Center.

"Okay?" he asked, hands open, looking down at his attire.

"Very good."

"The point being to look as if we belonged here."

"Two Yups, doing lunch."

"And the Bureau is paying," he whispered. "Of course."

"In your dreams."

She had a reservation in her own name, and they were ushered past a line of shoppers, drop-ins who frowned enviously as they went by. Kaufman's tailored jacket covered the callipygian behind but could not hide it. Briefly Bradford felt as if he were on a real date, with a grown-up woman.

"If someone you know sees you here," she said as they sat down, "what do you say?"

174

"You're my tax accountant."

"Good enough."

"What did you find out about the old guy in the Fillmore?"

"Nothing. He never reported it."

"Incredible."

She looked up at him. "You don't know much about black folk, do you?"

"I guess not."

Silence. Bradford gawked at the other patrons, smiling and well-dressed. Most were about his age. He supposed he had led a peculiar life.

"Briscoe surprised me," he said at last.

"Like I said: don't put anything past him."

"I won't."

"In one way he's been consistent. What he says he'll do, he does. If the pattern holds, this should be over pretty soon."

"Uh-huh."

"That should make you feel better."

"Give it a while to sink in."

When the waiter had take their orders, he asked, "To what do I owe the honor?"

"Mostly we just want to see how you're holding up."

"Oh."

"Well?"

"I suspect my blood pressure and resting heart rate are somewhat elevated. I sleep okay. Eat well."

"What about alcohol?"

"As much as usual. No more."

"As much as usual might be a little too much."

"That's what Briscoe says."

The waiter brought Michelob for him, Diet Coke for her.

"How's your head?"

"Could be better."

"Symptoms?"

"Paranoia, fluctuating between mild and moderate. Occasionally verging on extreme."

"Tell me more."

"I worry about being set-up."

"Wouldn't put it past them. But if you stay alert and keep in touch, you should be okay."

"Have you told the local cops to leave me alone?"

"We're in touch."

"Rumor has it that the Superintenden. is investigating me. Wants to boot me out of Hamilton. I can't remember if I told you."

"You didn't."

"It's hearsay, but probably reliable. Passed on by a colleague with connections at the central office."

"Who?"

"Joe Hensley."

She nodded. "I wouldn't worry about it Your central office doesn't kill people, right?"

"Not directly. You've heard of Hensley?"

"The name has come up."

"He has right-wing opinions."

"Yes."

"You think he's involved?"

"At this point we have no reason to think so. Do you?"

Bradford looked away. "No."

"Sure about that?"

"In these circumstances, anybody marginally to the right of Colin Powell makes me very, very nervous."

"That's all it is?"

"Yeah."

Their food arrived, and for a time they ate silently. Bradford had ordered Saltimbocca, and he soon realized the meal was better than any he could remember. He ate slowly, cleansing his palate with sips of beer. He ordered a non-alcoholic Klausthaler to replace the Michelob.

"This okay, Mom?" he asked, pointing to the new bottle.

"Excellent. Listen. There are two new wrinkles you need to know about. The first is that we have to focus on Briscoe, because he seems to be the honcho. The second is that, for your own sake, you need to be extra careful about Wilson."

"Why's that?"

"When he was twelve, he murdered his father."

"Terrific."

"It took us a while to find out because the juvenile record had been sealed. He's been clean ever since."

"Great. He really hates me."

"So you say. The problem is we can't watch either of you at school, and outside of school we can't watch him all the time. Our resources are limited."

"I don't suppose that in the circumstances I could get away with packing a little heat."

"No. You absolutely could not."

"Just thought I'd ask."

Bradford had heard of a rather nice hotel which supplemented the usual tourist trade by catering to adulterous couples checking in for nooners. If it had not been for the unpleasantness in the office suite south of Market, he might have extended an invitation to Ms. Kaufman. Now he considered a more modest overture, a bit of footsie, yet knew he wouldn't get away with that either. Wanting Kaufman and loving Molly did not, for some reason, seem at all inconsistent. He supposed he was more lonely than horny. He needed comfort.

He spent most of the Christmas recess alone, though Molly sent notes. One arrived on Christmas Eve, another just before New Years'. He had not authorized Kaufman's people to open his mail, and the envelopes did not appear to have been tampered with, but he worried nonetheless. Molly asked how he was doing, how he occupied himself. Though she did not seem angry about his call to her house, the messages in tone reminded him a bit of Cheryl Kaufman.

On Christmas Eve he got drunk, spent the holiday hung over. The next day he established a routine to get himself through the next week. In the morning he marked essays from seven to ten-thirty and then ran errands until lunch. He napped until three, worked out until dinner, and drank just enough during and after the meal to put himself to sleep. He masturbated twice a day, imagining himself with Molly or Cheryl Kaufman. All that time he dreaded the next call from Briscoe, but it did not come.

School resumed the day after New Years'. Albert stopped by between first and second periods to ask Bradford if he would be in the tutoring center later. The return to work had improved Bradford's spirits, but for some reason Albert's appearance began a reversal of the trend. Third period went badly. After lunch Bradford wandered the halls, hoping to catch a glimpse of Molly, but he did not see her. When he sat down with Albert, he was not in a good mood.

From a vanilla-colored folder Albert produced a set of white forms.

"What's all this?" Bradford asked.

"My uncle want to come here. I fill out forms. Can you see if I do right?

"Why are you doing them?"

Albert grinned. "In my fam'ly I know Eng-lish bes'." He laughed to show that he saw the irony.

"This isn't school work, Albert. I'm here to help you with schoolwork."

178

The boy pointed to the documents. "Is Eng-lish. You help, my Eng-lish get better."

Bradford set his jaw, stared at the papers. "Still, it's not schoolwork."

"Oh. Okay." Albert gathered up the papers, slid them back into the folder. Then he got up, looking embarrassed. "I don' need help wi' anything else today."

Bradford's pride required him to explain further. "I'm not an immigration worker, Albert. I'm not sure I even believe in it."

"Believe what?"

"In immigration."

"Oh. Okay."

When the boy had gone, Bradford sat still, his face hot with shame. Its source was not his stand on the issue but his cruelty in revealing it to the boy who, if he understood at all, would take it personally. Which it was, in a sense. Truly, Bradford wished they would all go back where they came from.

Softly, the CD player played Dvorak. *Symphony in E Minor: From the New World.*

During sixth period an announcement came over the public address system. The bus sent to take the girls' basketball team to Alameda had broken down. Gordon and the new AP's would cover the seventh period classes of teachers who would volunteer to drive the girls to and from the game. Bradford was on the intercom, calling Gordon, before the last word had been spoken. When he pulled up to the gym steps, Molly gave him a sober, measured look, as if he presented a problem she had not anticipated; but she and two others approached his car. Molly opened the back door.

"Get in front, Mol," said Anita Narvarez, the first-string point guard. "You got longer legs."

"I'm all right," said Molly.

In the rear-view mirror, however, Bradford could see that she had to scrunch up. He moved the front seat forward but still felt her knees, through it, against his spine. It occurred to him that perhaps she meant to make him uncomfortable.

It was a cold and rainy afternoon. Traffic on the Bay Bridge was heavy and slow, and Bradford got lost in Alameda. By the time they arrived the Hamilton coach had allowed the game to start, using second stringers, and Alameda had gone up, 15-4. The Hamilton girls closed the gap to 53-49 at the end of the third quarter, but Molly fouled out with seven minutes to go, and Alameda held on to win 70-68. Molly had gone six for twenty from the floor, three for seven from the line.

Going home, the girls were silent and sullen. When Bradford had negotiated the Alameda tunnel and the freeway ramp, he apologized.

"I cost you the game. I'm sorry."

"We didn't deserve to win," said Anita, beside him. "We played like shit."

"They looked like a pretty good club," said Bradford.

"No way," said Cindy Henderson, in back beside Molly. She was Hamilton's only black player, sister of the wayward Leticia, who had quit school in November.

"Well, anyway," said Bradford. "It was non-league."

"Yeah," said Anita, "but we lose our ranking."

"Win the league, and Nor-Cal, and you get it back."

This analysis was indisputable, but it was no comfort to the girls, who did not respond. Despite his guilt Bradford began to enjoy the smell of warm, sweaty females. No one spoke again until they left the off-ramp in the city.

"Okay, Ladies. Who lives where?"

Bradford dropped Anita and Seventeenth and Sanchez, Cindy at Pine and Divisadero. Molly did not speak until

Bradford pulled into a bus stop on Jackson Street a block from her house. It was raining again. Trees blocked light from the streetlamp, and when Bradford turned to look he could barely make out her features.

"Anita's gonna figure it out."

"Figure out what?"

"That something's going on with us."

"Why do you think that?"

"Because you should have taken me and Cindy home first. Anita <u>knows</u> you live over there. She sees you all the time."

"Maybe I wasn't planning to go straight home. Maybe I have an engagement elsewhere."

Suddenly Molly got out of the car. Then yanked open the passenger door, got in beside him. She sat up straight with her knees tight together, scowling.

"Thought you were leaving."

"Why should I leave? You're my boyfriend, right? My red-hot lover!"

"Wow. You <u>are</u> pissed."

"Why shouldn't I be? That was the <u>worst</u> fucking game I ever played!"

"Come on. You were way behind when you went in. You didn't even get to warm up."

"That doesn't explain the second half."

"Okay. You had a bad day. All athletes have them, as I should not have to tell you."

Molly did not reply.

"Am I right?"

"Are you any closer to be through with that stuff?"

"I don't know. I haven't heard from anybody lately."

After a moment she said, "My life is so <u>weird</u>! So <u>abnormal</u>!"

"In . . . one dimension it is."

"How'm I supposed to separate you from the rest of it?"

181

"You have to try."

"I do. It doesn't work."

For a time neither spoke.

"In Miss Wetherall's class we're reading *Ulysses*. So you know what the kids call me?"

"Molly Bloom."

"Yes."

"Simply because your name is Molly."

"How do I <u>know</u> that? Maybe they know I'm this horny, adulterous female?"

"You have to be married to be adulterous."

"No you don't. It also means 'all manner of lewdness or unchastity.'"

"That definition is archaic. Nobody—"

"—Never mind!"

"Okay."

After a moment she took his hand.

"I'm sorry. I'm being this real bitch. But it's <u>hard</u>."

She let her head fall back slightly, closed her eyes. After a moment she said, "Know what? I was nominated for Prom Queen."

"I saw that, in the bulletin. Good for you."

"You think that's really, really stupid."

"No. I don't."

"It <u>is</u> really stupid. I know that. But it was sort of nice to know not <u>everybody</u> thinks I'm just this overgrown dyke jock."

"Nobody sees you—"

"—Shut up a minute!. And so I think, what if I got elected, and then everybody found out what we're doing? What a joke. People would remember for the rest of their fucking <u>lives</u>."

"You are a wee bit overwrought."

"Oh, fuck you! Take me home!"

"Have you changed your mind? Do you want to call it quits?"

Molly did not answer this question. But after a moment she said, "I'll be eighteen in five and a half weeks."

"Yeah. By itself though, that—"

"—We could get married."

"Yes."

"Then they couldn't get you for statutory whatever. We could be together."

"Yes."

"Would you do that?"

"In an instant."

"Even though I'm still, like, this <u>child</u>. Even if you were <u>ruining</u> my life."

"I told you once that I can go only so far on the basis of moral principle."

"What does that mean, exactly?"

"That I would marry you in the hope that you would be happy, knowing full well that it might be bad for you."

After a moment she said, "Sometimes you scare me."

"No surprise. I'm a selfish bastard, obviously."

"It's not that."

"What, then?"

She thought for a moment. Then she said, "That you're grown-up."

"Are selfish people grown-up?"

"What I mean is, you've lived <u>twice</u> as long as I have. I don't have any idea what that's <u>like</u>."

Bradford nodded.

"Do you understand?"

"Yes."

A moment later she leaned toward him, put an arm around his neck.

"Give me a kiss," she said. "And then take me home."

He did.

183

SEVENTEEN

Two nights later Briscoe called to say that he had the pistol. He suggested they go to the gun range. Bradford agreed, called Kaufman, and quickly activated a listening device which one of her colleagues had planted in a living room lamp.

Bradford had not seen Briscoe in more than a month and was startled by his appearance. He wore faded jeans, a newish denim jacket, a beige cowboy hat with a snakeskin band, and boots with pointy toes. Bradford stared at him; and, despite all that had happened, again wondered if any of this could be quite serious.

"Well. Howdy, Pard."

Briscoe smirked. "Been doin' stuff with Bob. I thought we oughta look like we belong together."

"It suits you."

"Means to an end."

Briscoe carried a small black plastic case. He sat on Bradford's sofa, unlocked its tiny padlock with a tinier key. He opened the case, handed the pistol to Bradford.

"Looks like a toy."

"It's no toy. But in your pocket it'll look like a wallet."

"Do I give you a check?"

"We'll stop at your ATM. You give me what cash you can get now, the rest later."

"Okay." Bradford stood up, slipped the weapon into his pocket.

"No. You carry it unloaded and in the case."

"I didn't know we were so law-abiding."

"Oh yeah. We're good citizens."

After a stop at Bradford's bank they drove to Hot Shot, the gun range in South City. On the way they spoke only once.

"Can you believe that fuckin' nigger got elected?"

"I was surprised."

"I almost went nuts. Loaded all my guns and just sat there lookin' at 'em. Hardly slept for two nights."

Hot Shot was a low-slung concrete building in a small industrial park. Its showroom was clean and cheery with new lime paint, white acoustical ceiling tile, wall-to-wall carpet, and fluorescent lighting. There were aluminum racks for gun cases, books, paper targets, and cleaning equipment. Weapons gleamed in locked glass display cabinets. Through a broad window at the rear Bradford could see men on range, hear the muffled snap and crack of gunfire.

At a counter before the window the rangemaster inspected their weapons. To his left, looking bored, stood a young man in a white dress shirt and jeans; in a belt holster he carried a 9 mm. automatic. Briscoe and Bradford filled out printed cards--orders for targets, ammunition, and ear-protectors. After providing these items the rangemaster took their drivers' licenses, clipped them to the cards, put them in a file box.

They entered a small chamber between the showroom and the range.

"Put on the guards."

"Why's he want our licenses?"

"So they'll know where to send the body if you shoot yourself."

"Who's the guy with the automatic?"

"Security. Usually they're cops, moonlighting."

"Don't we wanna avoid cops?"

"They know me anyway. It's a chance we have to take."

Bradford started and winced as the door to the range closed behind them. Even with ear guards the explosions were stunning and painful.

Briscoe grinned, clapped him on the back, and shouted.

"Not used to this, uh?"

Bradford shook his head. They stepped into a cubicle between concrete walls. Before them was a wood counter and beyond it the range itself, about fifty yards deep. When they had set the gear on the counter, Briscoe pointed to buttons set in the wall beside Bradford.

"Push the lower one!"

Bradford did, then sensed faint vibrations. Just overhead, wires began to move: a trolley. Briscoe showed him how to attach his target, the silhouette of a man from the waist up, and send it halfway down range. They removed their weapons from the cases, loaded them. Briscoe demonstrated the cup-and-saucer grip, but Bradford had trouble concentrating. The noise kept making him start and blink. The acrid smell of burnt powder waxed and waned. Bradford realized that his hands were sweating.

Briscoe fired a clip at his target, spacing his shots precisely, one every three seconds. Then he changed the clip and set his pistol on the counter.

"Now you," he shouted.

Bradford wiped his hands on the back of his pants, yet felt heat and moisture again even as he reached for his weapon. Taking his stance, bending his knees, locking his elbow, cupping the heel of his shooting hand in the palm of the other, sighting on the target, he felt completely incompetent and utterly ridiculous. As he squeezed off the first shot, his damp forefinger seemed to slip on the trigger.

When he had finished the clip, he pushed the button, brought back the targets. Briscoe's group was tight at the center of the silhouette. One of Bradford's shots had nicked the left shoulder, another the right ear. To his surprise, the rest were reasonably well centered.

"Not bad!" shouted Briscoe. He snapped Bradford's target with a forefinger. "He is one dead motherfucker."

Bradford stared at the riddled paper.

Briscoe shouted again. "We'll call him . . . "

"What?"

Again Briscoe shouted, but this time Bradford heard nothing.

As Briscoe's mouth moved once again, Bradford inclined his head and, with thumb and forefingers, lifted the cups of the earguards.

"Freddy Lamar! Don't—"

There were two overlapping explosions. Bradford spun to his right as if struck.

Briscoe had him by the arm. He was yelling, and Bradford seemed to read his lips. "NEVER DO THAT, MAN!"

Briscoe pulled him from the cubicle, into the chamber between the range and the showroom.

When they had removed the guards, Briscoe said, "Can you hear?"

Bradford nodded.

"Ears ringing?"

"Yeah." His voice sounded small and distant.

"That's a good sign. But if it doesn't stop in a week or so, you'll need to get yourself checked out."

Again Bradford nodded.

The rangemaster opened the other door. He looked at Bradford, then at Briscoe.

"We're all right," said Briscoe. The rangemaster backed out and shut the door.

"Man, you never do that. Why did you?"

"I guess I forgot where we were."

Briscoe stared at him. "You gotta have presence of mind."

"Yeah." Bradford swallowed several times, hoping, stupidly, to lessen the ringing.

"You game for more?"

"Yeah."

On the range Bradford fired off three more clips. His head ached, his ears rang, his hands sweat. But he did about as well as before.

When they reached the car, Briscoe said, "You don't look so good."

"I'm okay."

"That happened to me once. I was firing a .44 Magnum outdoors, and this asshole came up behind me and lifted my guards just as I fired. He thought it was funny."

"Not funny."

"Fuckin' A. I split his lip, right there." Briscoe unlocked the passenger side door. "Anyway—I like the way you went right back at it."

On the way to the city they were silent. The din in Bradford's ears held steady. When they stopped in the front of the house, he started to get out,

"Wait."

Bradford looked at him. Shut the door.

"The time has come."

Briscoe sounded far away.

"Oh."

"The actions will take place a week from Monday. The day Nigger Freddy gets inaugurated."

"We gonna hit him?"

Briscoe smiled faintly. "That appeal to you?"

Bradford shrugged.

"Sure does to me. Problem is, it'd be a suicide mission. I'm not ready for that. Not yet."

"So?"

"So we take out his key flunkies."

"Oh."

"Your assignment will be a greaseball cunt named Rosalia Fernandez."

"The lawyer."

"Right."

"I'd rather go after a man."

"Evil has no sex."

Bradford did not reply.

"You committed yourself, Mickey."

"All right. Where do I find her?"

"She leaves home every weekday morning at eight-fifteen. Walks to work. You just pick a quiet block, come up behind her, and blow her fucking head off."

"Okay."

"Got a different car for you, too."

"That Falcon?"

"Yeah. You pick it up the night before."

"Uh-huh. Who else are we after?"

"That you read about in the papers."

Bradford nodded.

"We're gonna make history, Mickey. Someday we'll be as famous as Oswald."

"I thought we weren't gonna get caught."

"I mean after the war. The movement will need leaders. Heroes."

"Uh-huh." Bradford gazed through the windshield, up States to the bend in the street. The guy believed it. Every word.

"We'll change things forever. How many people do that?"

Bradford did not reply.

"You hands sweat pretty bad. Was it after you hurt your ears?"

Bradford nodded.

"Good. This wasn't to prepare you for Fernandez, you know. You can stick the fuckin' barrel in her ear. This was in case somebody comes after you. A cop or whoever."

"Okay."

Briscoe grinned at him. "Don't worry. You'll make a real gunslinger, eventually."

"Whatever you say."

"Between now and then, take it easy on the booze."

"All right."

Briscoe paused.

"Somethin' else I been meanin' to ask you."

"Uh-huh."

"I sort of took it for granted that you're between women, like me."

"Yeah."

"Wynnie thinks you got something goin' with some big girl at school. Says he sees you with her."

Bradford shook his head. "We just flirt. I have fantasies about her."

"Fantasies."

"I imagine doing nasty things to her tender young flesh."

Briscoe laughed. "Hell, go do 'em. But not till this is over."

Again Bradford shook his head. "She's jailbait."

"Okay. Just wanted to be sure. Goin' into somethin' like this, you don't wanna be moonin' over some twat at the same time."

"Yeah."

"Just try and relax."

"Right."

Later Bradford got drunk in his father's den. His ears kept ringing. In bed he lay sleepless. He wondered if going deaf would be a fair price for an end to all this.

Kaufman had told him not to call right after meeting Briscoe. The next morning, after seeing Wilson at work on the third floor, Bradford went downstairs and entered the scarred wooden phone booth in the lobby.

"I don't like this much," he told Kaufman. "He wouldn't say a word at my place."

"Suspicion is part of the game."

"Game?"

"For them it is a game..Till they get themselves in deep shit, that is. Do I have to tell you you're dealing with cases of arrested development?"

Bradford sighed.

"Just be careful."

Kaufman seemed far away, light years beyond the ringing in his ears.

"You think this is for real."

"So far it checks out."

"How does it check out?"

"I'd rather not get into that."

"You sound just like Briscoe!" Bradford was nearly shouting. "I'm putting my ass on the line to avoid jail, but I begin to wonder if it's a good trade."

Kaufman hesitated, then said, "He's been scouting, he and the old guy. On Rosalia Fernandez' block, among other places."

"You know who the other targets are?"

"Some, maybe. They go someplace, we check on who lives in the neighborhood, make our inferences. But we can't be sure."

Bradford shut his eyes. He felt desperate. He wanted to tell her about Molly.

"We're on them twenty-four hours a day now. No matter who they go after, we should be able to stop them."

"Happy to hear it."

"Just play along. Don't ask him any more questions."

"All right."

"Try and relax."

That night, as he dressed for bed, it occurred to him that his talks with Briscoe and Kaufman had ended with the same words. He caught sight of himself in the bureau mirror and thought, Pawn to Queen four.

EIGHTEEN

Bradford slept badly that night, taught poorly the next day. Quotidian failure in the classroom deepened his loneliness and pushed him over one of the various edges surrounding him. He visited Joe Hensley, whom he had been avoiding.

As usual, the Colonel was at his desk. He did nearly all his work at school, sometimes staying till six or seven. This was simply one more of his exemplary practices. Bradford, since his demotion, left precisely at three-fifteen and took his papers home, where they nagged at him, haunted him.

"Mickey. Haven't seen you lately."

"Yeah. How you been?"

The room had a faintly fruity smell. The day's banana peels and apple cores, rotting in the wastebaskets.

"Well enough. Thinking about retirement."

Bradford shook his head. "You say that every spring. They'll have to carry you out of here."

"No. I don't think so."

"You going to this forum on Saturday?"

"With reluctance. I'm on the panel."

"With who else?"

"Gordon, Gwen, Janie, and Lucille."

"Seems like a waste of time."

"What is the current phrase? 'It's a girl thing.'"

Bradford laughed.

"Perfectly intelligent and experienced women—and they still think those people can be persuaded."

"Yeah."

"You're not coming?"

"No. I'm one of the villains, remember. I'd just set people off."

"What do you hear of the Supe's nefarious intentions? Regarding yourself."

"Nothing."

"Good."

"Listen. Have you had any more little notes from Ones and Twos?"

"No."

Bradford nodded.

"But you have."

"I've . . . heard from them. How'd you know?"

"Your manner, Sir, is most portentous."

Bradford laughed. "Is it?"

Hensley gazed at him. "You seem . . . wound up."

"I guess I am."

"Well?"

"In the strictest confidence, Colonel."

"Of course."

"They contacted me. Wilson is involved, and at least two others. They're the people who made all that noise at the Board meeting. And cut the lights. They killed Shabazz' dog, and I think they beat up Rohrer, but I don't know for sure."

The Colonel continued to gaze at him. He had turned off his desk lamp, and his face was in shadow. "And what have you done?"

"Shapley's car."

"You did that?"

"Yeah."

Hensley nodded.

"There are other things I can't tell you about."

Silence.

"We go back a long way, Colonel. I was wondering what you'd think."

"There's more in the offing."

"I think so."

"And you're having doubts?"

"Wouldn't you?"

"Certainly."

"Well?"

"I can't _advise_ you, Mick?"

"Thoughtful commentary would be appreciated."

Hensley clasped his hands, turned his head. Seemed to gaze out the window. "The school is lost, you know."

"You think so?"

"Yes. That's why I picked up retirement papers."

"Your reliable source again?"

"Yes. So—before you get yourself into further difficulties . . . "

"I see."

For a moment neither spoke.

"On the other hand, there's always something to be said for going down swinging."

Bradford raised one hand in a theatrical gesture. "'A man does not fight only to win!'"

"What's that from?"

"_Cyrano de Bergerac._"

"I always meant to read that."

"Old Cyrano, he wasted guys right and left. Mostly offstage and between lyrical improvisations."

"Bad guys, I presume."

"Yeah." Bradford studied the still face.

"Wasting is certainly an issue."

"Yeah."

The Colonel did not reply at once. Then he said, "There are bad guys involved here. As we know."

"Yeah."

"I presume Cyrano thought about that."

"I guess he did. I don't remember."

"Well. That's the extent of my thoughtful commentary."

Bradford stood up. "Fair enough."

At the door Bradford turned to look at the Colonel, but he had returned to his papers. Bradford could hear the heel of his hand move across them. Whish . . . whish . . . whish.

Bradford had half-intended to ask the Colonel, flat out, if he knew Briscoe and Big Bob. In the end he was afraid to know.

Before dinner Bradford punched the bag until he was tired. At dinner and in the evening he drank moderately. He watched ESPN until ten o'clock, when he called the District's voicemail to say that he was ill and would be in on Wednesday. He had decided he needed a day to think. In bed he lay awake until one. Then he took Sominex and slept nearly ten hours.

In the morning he shaved and dressed, drank coffee, and then, to shake the antihistamine hangover, climbed Corona Heights to Red Rock. Once again the weather was inappropriately bright and cheerful. He could see to Mt. Diablo and beyond. After a light lunch he made more coffee and retired to the den and the recliner.

Very soon he understood that he had not needed a day off. The relevant facts were few, their relations limited. His options were clear fifteen minutes after he had sat down. Nevertheless, he spent more than an hour in the recliner, considering and reconsidering.

The problem was whether or not to call Kaufman and ask her to provide protection for Molly. The mere fact that Briscoe knew something of his connection to her was enough to make Bradford put his hand on the receiver again and again. There was simply no telling how <u>much</u> Briscoe knew. Wilson might have noted, and spoken of, the long hour in the gymnasium.

Why should it matter to them?

No reason now. Later, after they knew he had betrayed them, things might be different. Even if they had no actual accomplices, they had friends in the movement. Word would get out. He himself could become a marked man, and it seemed by no means impossible that people might go after anyone they thought he cared about.

Still. Gut feeling said that Briscoe had believed his explanation of the matter. If he had, there was nothing to worry about.

Yes. He was being paranoid. Besides, even the fucking Mafia didn't kill women and children. And if he called Kaufman, now he would have to tell her everything. Molly would be questioned, even called as a witness.

At last Bradford rose, went to his desk, and wrote his monthly checks, sealed the envelopes and stamped them. Then he walked over the hill to Cole Valley, mailing the bills on the way. In a gourmet deli he bought potato salad, avocado salad, and spare ribs. He also bought a twenty-one dollar bottle of Cabernet Sauvignon. At home, though sore from his last workout, he punched the bag for nearly an hour. The he showered, dressed, heated the spare ribs, and sat down to eat.

Though he could recall no specific instances, he knew that obscenely rich food sometimes gave him an hour's pleasant distraction, respite from grief and trouble. It did not; but the wine, of course, always did. He drank the entire bottle and retired to the den with a glass of brandy. Soon he was thinking about the two loaded weapons upstairs, hidden in an empty Kleenex box.

He could drive to Briscoe's and kill him. Drive to Wilson's, blow him away too. That left Big Bob. Bradford got up, padded into the hallway to get the telephone book. Drunk and barefoot, he tended to lean back as he walked, put weight on his heels. Someday he would just topple over backward. He could smell his own liquory breath.

Big Bob was not in the book. Bradford supposed that no one in the Movement would be. There might aliases, but not real names. In the moment this supposition seemed profound, Holmesian, definitely consequential; he tested it, looking up Briscoe and Wilson. Both were there, with full names and addresses. Bradford felt silly.

No matter. If he killed Wilson and Briscoe, he would go prison for the rest of his life, but the conspiracy would be over. Everyone would believe that he had simply lost his mind. No one would bother Molly.

Or would they?

He was now too drunk to figure it out.

It would be safer and simpler to kill himself. That little event wouldn't even make the papers, though it might alarm the Feds. But he could do it here, in the recliner. His fingerprints would be on the weapon. There would be powder burns as well. End of investigation. Briscoe and the others would fear implication and stay far away from anyone having to do with Michael T. Bradford, recently deceased.

Michael T. Bradford, still among the living, arose and went unsteadily upstairs. In his room he sat down on the bed, leaned forward, tugged open the drawer of the bedside table. As he reached into the box for the automatic, his hands were already sweating. And once he held it in his hand he was again quite sure—he had somehow forgotten—that he would never kill himself. Whatever was done to him would be done by others.

He removed the clip from the automatic and the cartridges from the revolver. Hands still perspiring, he carried them to the basement, where he placed them, without knowing why, in the drawer of his father's old workbench.

As he climbed the kitchen steps, the telephone rang.

"Hello."

"Hi. It's me."

"Yes."

"I'm all alone for two days. I want you to come over and knock me up."

"I can't talk now. I'll call you back."

"You better."

Bradford got his jacket, walked to the Twin Peaks Tavern. It was a slow night, but one guy gave him that *fresh meat* look. Staring him down, Bradford dialed Molly's number.

"What's up, Girl?"

"I told you what's up."

"You're not on the pill?"

"I haven't taken it since I knew they were going."

"Is this a rational considered decision?"

"No."

"Pregnancy would affect your rebounding."

"I could take a year off."

"You're crazy."

"Just come over. I want you here."

"I'd be followed, I think."

"Why would they do that on a school night? Before anything is supposed to happen?"

Bradford hesitated. "I think they would."

"I think you're paranoid."

"I think you're reckless."

"I don't care if my name's in the paper."

"You cared last month."

"Mickey, come over here."

"You wouldn't want to see me. I'm half-tanked."

"What?"

"I'm half-tanked. Maybe three-quarters."

"You mean you're <u>drunk</u>?"

"Partly."

"Do you drink a <u>lot</u>?"

"Sometimes."

"I thought you sounded a little funny."

"I'm sorry."

"I've never seen you do it."

"When we're together I have better things to do."

"I have an uncle who drinks. He passes out at family dinners. Do you do that?"

"No."

"What do you do?"

"I blow up cars sometimes."

"You were drunk when you did that?"

"Didn't I tell you?"

"No. You just said you met the guys in a bar."

"Oh."

Silence.

"I guess I don't want you here if you're drunk."

"I could get sober fast, but that's not the point. Listen, Mol. I told you once these guys might be dangerous. Now there's no <u>might</u> about it."

"How do you know?"

"I was there when one of 'em tried to kill somebody."

"Really?"

"Yeah. All this is coming to a head. We absolutely can't talk again till it's over. Not even at school."

"What's going to happen?"

"I can't tell you that."

"Well. I can't stand this." She started to cry. "I need to talk to somebody."

Bradford sighed. "Who?"

Molly sobbed, caught her breath. "My parents."

In that moment Bradford, cold sober, decided that he truly deserved to go to jail for statutory rape.

"Okay. Tell them. But not till next week. For reasons that don't have anything to do with us."

"All right."

"Good. That's all I need."

"They won't prosecute you, Mickey. I know them."

"Fine. But that's the least of my problems at the moment. Do you understand?"

"Yes."

"Okay. Get some sleep now."

"All right."

When Bradford got home, the phone was ringing.

"Hello, Cheryl."

"I understand you had an interesting phone call."

"Personal business. An old girl friend."

"That we can't know about."

"You got it. I'm not airing dirty laundry for the entertainment of your night man."

"You have bigger problems than dirty laundry."

"The woman is in a sensitive position."

"Married?"

"She has a jealous and violent lover."

Bradford was pleased to reflect that he was telling the literal truth. Kaufman did not reply at once.

"Listen. Personally, I'm inclined to believe you. I think you're a messy guy with a messy life. But I don't run the show, and my bosses won't like this. Believe me."

"Let the chips fall."

"Okay. Good night."

NINETEEN

On Thursday night Briscoe called. He told Bradford to shop where no one knew him, pay cash, and acquire clothes different from any in which he had been seen. Bradford welcomed the distraction of this task. On Friday after school he drove to the Serramonte mall and bought an A's cap, sunglasses, and a nondescript green windbreaker. Afterward he had a beer in the food court and watched the girls go by. He had just arrived home when Briscoe called again.

"Get the stuff?"

"Yeah."

"Good. Be home at ten tomorrow morning. I got a little somethin' else for you."

"Fake glasses and big nose."

"Hey, pretty close. Don't forget. Ten o'clock."

Bradford drove to the Marina district, where he called Kaufman from the parking lot at I-Hop to be sure she knew about Briscoe's impending visit. During a dinner of pancakes, eggs, and sausage, which he regarded as only the first of the condemned man's rich and unhealthy last meals, he thought about changing his plan for the evening. The

Hamilton girls were playing that night in San Mateo. No reason why he couldn't go.

But he didn't. He went instead to a film, *Sense and Sensibility* at the Cinema 21. In the chilly evening air he waited near the end of a long line among good-looking people his own age. They were exuberant in release from the week's work, and he registered the fragments of their lives: names and Sunday brunches, bike tours and triathlons, weekend getaways and vacations in Cabo, resumes and job hunts. He had never been so lonely.

The theater was unpleasant, and right away he wished he had gone to the game. From his corner seat in the third row the huge images were slanted and distorted. The smell of stale butter pervaded, and beneath his feet he felt rubbery popcorn and the stickiness of spilled drinks. He remembered that his briefcase was a jumble of papers, his house a shambles. He kept noticing the skin blemishes of the actors. Yet eventually the film caught him, freed him, and as Emma Thompson wept in the final scene, he too wept.

Outside the theater the spell passed. Driving home, he knew he would not sleep. On Franklin Street, near the Unitarian Church, he happened to see a car pulling out of a space. On an impulse he parked and walked down the hill to the O'Farrell Theater, where he paid an admission price of twenty dollars and, in a darkened room, watched a young woman fuck herself with a huge vibrator as nine invisible men focused flashlight beams on her distended vulva. When she had faked her orgasm, Bradford let his light pass quickly over her face and hair. She was a strawberry blonde and, though she blinked and scowled in the sudden light, much prettier than Molly, Cheryl Kaufman, or Emma Thompson. He wondered at the ways of the world.

With the rest he went to a larger room to see four other quite lovely girls simulate cunnilingus on what appeared to be a large wrestling mat. Their singly splendid bodies became a grotesque, trembling, goose-pimpled octopus. From the doorway of a small auditorium he watched a tall redhead dance naked on stage and keep losing the beat. A tiny Japanese girl approached him, grinning with teeth outsized but otherwise flawless. Beneath her translucent bra she had nipples the size of half-dollars. She offered to gyrate on his lap and send him home with sticky pants. He declined the offer and left.

At nine the next morning Bradford was still in pajamas and slippers. Brutal sunshine on his face and beard drove him from the den to the dim and musty living room, where he drank a second mug of coffee and read the paper in soothing electric light. At last he went upstairs to shave, dress, and do some stretching before Briscoe arrived. He felt stiff and elderly, vulnerable in pajamas and bare feet. His balls lung loose. Even lightweight shoes could crush his toes.

The doorbell rang at exactly ten o'clock.

Briscoe stepped quickly into the foyer, and Bradford saw that there had been another metamorphosis. The mustache and hair were short and neat, the face pink from the razor. The cotton pants and shirt were of identical olive green. Just above the breast pocket of the shirt, an oval namepatch had been cut away.

"So," said Bradford. "Whaddya got?"

"Huh?" Briscoe raised his eyebrows slightly, as if he had forgotten why he had come. "Oh."

From his breast pocket he removed a small item wrapped in Kleenex. He held the tissue by one corner, above his left hand, and let it unroll. Into his palm dropped a fake mustache.

"Oh, Man. Gimme a break."

"You need it. It'll change you more than anything else."

205

Bradford made a face. He picked up the bristly thing, reminded of caterpillars.

"Get the rest of your stuff, Mickey. We're going now."

"What?"

"We have new targets, and we all go together."

"You're kidding."

"Nope."

"Why?"

"Logistical reasons, mostly."

The hard g again. "This is crazy."

"Don't argue. Get your stuff."

Bradford did not move.

"When you've been with us a while, you'll expect this kinda thing. Now come on."

Bradford turned on his heel and headed upstairs. The announcement had startled him, but slowly a simple and exhilarating thought took form and made him tingle: it would all be over soon. In the upstairs hallway he remembered that Kaufman had told him to take the phone off the hook in an emergency. He got his jacket, cap, and pistol. Then lifted the receiver, laid it on the night stand.

Downstairs again, he said, "Clip's in the basement."

"Why?"

"I had this dream," said Bradford, heading for the door to the basement steps. "I shot myself in the middle of the night."

"So?" Briscoe was following.

"I was afraid I'd sleepwalk and really do it."

"Shit. How spooked are you?"

"Spooked enough." Bradford marveled at his own imagination.

"You shoulda told me. I coulda got you somethin' to take."

"Ready for anything, uh?"

"My business to be."

Briscoe's car smelled of cigarette smoke. Bradford asked where they were going.

"Later. The less time you have to think—"

"—the better I'll do. Yada, yada, yada."

"No yada."

For a while neither spoke. Bradford's exhilaration had passed. Suppose Kaufman's people lost them again? He checked the rear-view every block or so. She had told him that they sometimes used a blue Honda, but he did not see one.

In front of a shabby hotel on Jones Street Briscoe stopped and honked. Bradford saw Big Bob sitting at a table in the lobby with two other elderly men. All read sections of the morning <u>Chronicle</u>. Big Bob looked up and saw them. He put down his newspaper and picked a white plastic bag. Through it Bradford could make out the dark square shape of a gun case.

"I thought he wasn't gonna be involved."

"Change of plans."

Bob got into the back seat, groaning. "Too fuckin' old for this shit."

When he had pulled away from the curb, Briscoe looked at Bradford.

"Okay, Mickey. Listen carefully. We're gonna change vehicles, and you're gonna drive."

"All right. But what the fuck are we doing?"

"Just hold on. Even Bob doesn't know. Right, Bob?"

"Right."

Bradford did not believe this.

"You thought Ones and Twos was bullshit, didn't you?"

"What?"

"I mean the concepts," said Briscoe. He sat up straight and frowned, assuming his <u>Commandante</u> manner. Sunlight gleamed on the clear skin of his high, faceted brow. "Leaderless resistance. Small units. High security."

"I thought you were the leader."

"This time! This time I am! Next time it could be you or Bob or even Wynnie!"

"God forbid."

"John Law fears conspiracy. But it ain't conspiracy he's up against here. It's what's in my head, and no way can he know what it is!"

"Pure anarchy."

"Not at all. Because the purpose is shared. And when we've blown it all apart, we'll organize and make a government."

"Who gives the signal for that?"

"The signal will be chaos."

Briscoe slowed, made a right into the public garage at Fifth and Mission. Headed up the corkscrew ramp, fast, and pulled into a parking space on the fourth floor.

"Now. We head for the elevator. But we get into that brown van, right there." Briscoe pointed. "It's unlocked. The keys'll be under the visor, Mickey. You start the vehicle and wait for instructions."

The garage was cool and shadowy. The slamming of the car doors echoed, the footsteps too. Bradford realized the others wore boots. He looked at his Nikes and thought *Yuppie scum.* In the wide space of concrete pillar and oil-stained pavement he looked for Kaufman's people but saw no one.

At the battered van Briscoe said, "Put on the jacket, Mickey."

Bradford did, then got in. The old bucket seats were split, showing yellow foam. Briscoe and Big Bob entered on the passenger side, slid between the seats and into the back. Bradford found the keys, started the engine, then reached down to adjust the seat. The last driver had very short legs. Who?

Briscoe spoke from the rear darkness.

"Now the mustache. Use the mirror."

Bradford took the thing from his pocket, positioned it beneath his nose, pressed it on. He felt ridiculous.

"Cap and shades."

Bradford put them on.

"Turn around."

He did. The men in the rear laughed.

"Your mother wouldn't know you," said Briscoe. "Now—the parking ticket and the money to pay are in the glove compartment. Take 'em out and put 'em on the seat beside you."

There was a <u>thunk</u> when Bradford put the van in reverse. Another when he went to low.

"Shit, Harley. This is a junker."

"It'll get us there and back. Don't worry."

Back on Mission Briscoe told him to head for Ninth Street.

"Remember: you're the safest fuckin' driver ever was."

"Yeah."

Bradford was too warm in the jacket, for it was another fine day, clear and brilliant. Without moving his head he checked side streets and the side mirrors, trying to fix certain vehicles in memory. None seemed to follow or re-appear.

Before his high school games they had screamed at each other, smacked pads and helmets in the tunnel before going on the field. The theory was that noise and pain helped get them ready. Now he reached back and slapped himself at the base of his skull.

"Whaddya doin'?" asked Briscoe.

"Tryin' to wake up."

A few minutes later, from the darkness, Big Bob spoke in a voice Bradford may not have been intended to hear. "I don't make anybody."

"Neither do I."

Bradford disliked being left out. "You can't be sure," he said.

"That's right, Mickey. We can't. But you did understand this might be a little bit dangerous. Right?"

Bradford did not reply. He considered shooting them. At the next light he put the vehicle in neutral. Pull the gun, turn, and start firing. The moment he thought of this his hands became moist. And they were far back, in pitch darkness. Probably watching him.

Bradford crossed Market on Ninth.

"Take Hayes and then Fell," said Briscoe. Suddenly he slid between the seats, sat beside Bradford.

"You all right now?"

"Wasn't I all right?"

"I don't know. Are you?"

"Yeah."

Briscoe said nothing.

"Why the change in plans?"

Briscoe hesitated. "A couple funny things happened this week. I could be under surveillance. If I am, they've figured out who we were after. So we throw 'em a curve."

"How?"

After a moment Briscoe began to giggle.

Without knowing quite why, Bradford grew furious.

"Harley. You tell me what's going on, or I'm getting out at the next light."

Bradford was applying the brakes when Briscoe finally replied.

"Me and Bob are gonna hit that meeting at Hamilton. We kill every nigger and greaseball we can."

Bradford went cold. He had forgotten the Forum entirely.

"That's crazy."

"Not at all. Best idea I ever had. When it's done, people will think we were pointin' toward it all along."

"Harley. If you think they're on to you, we oughta cool it and lie low for a while."

"No. I could be imagining things. The surveillance, I mean. And I've waited too goddamn long."

"Shit!"

A large calloused hand gripped Bradford's shoulder. He felt breath on his neck.

"Listen, school-boy. Just listen."

"Nobody's gonna recognize you," said Briscoe. "You're in disguise, and when we open fire you're four blocks away. All you have to do is be there when we come out."

Bradford was still hearing Big Bob. Something in the voice that had been there all along. That hadn't registered.

"It's gonna be mostly white people, Harley!"

"Well. They got nothin' to worry about. 'cept your buddy Rohrer."

"Look. Because of what happened to him, there're gonna be cops."

"Maybe. Maybe not, with all this inauguration shit goin' on. We avoid 'em if we can, blow 'em away if we can't."

"Jesus."

"All you gotta do about cops, School-boy, is surprise 'em," said Big Bob. "What good did cops do Kennedy?"

"Right. We'll be in and out so fast they won't know what hit 'em. Wynnie's set it up."

"Wilson?"

"Your head janitor picked him to work the meeting. How 'bout that? Another reason for the change."

"I have friends there."

Briscoe turned to look at him. "Nigger friends? Greaseballs?"

Bradford had no reply.

"I showed you I could shoot, didn't I?"

"Yes."

"Okay. Bob's better'n me, take my word for it. We move down the aisles, fire off one clip each, and fifteen or twenty mud people buy the farm. Nobody else unless they interfere."

Bradford found he could not speak.

"An' I tell ya what. For sure I get your old girlfriend Shabazz. I promised Wynnie an' he just about came in his pants."

Suddenly Briscoe looked over his shoulder. "You know what the kid wanted me to do? Bob?"

Big Bob grunted.

"He wanted me to rub the bullets in garlic, then just shoot her in the legs. He said she'd die of agony, of blood poisoning!"

"I never heard uh that."

"No, Listen!" Briscoe began to laugh, and for perhaps ten seconds he could not stop. "He read about it in a comic book!"

"Aw, Jesus," said Bob.

"Honest to God! I swear it!"

A minute later Briscoe spoke again. "Okay, Mickey. Listen up. You drop us off on Grove, behind the school. You make a right at the next block, go to Fulton. Go left on Fulton, keep takin' lefts. Around the hospital, back to Grove. Then double park someplace for a couple minutes. In exactly _five_ minutes, you're back where you started, behind the school."

"All right."

"Say it like you mean it!"

Bradford had just noticed that Briscoe had no seat belt.

212

"I mean it."

"One moh thing, <u>School</u>-boy."

Again Bradford felt the calloused hand.

"You be sure and be there."

"He'll be there."

"Youah in command, Hahley. But I want a little in-put at this point. If you ain't there, Schoolboy, an' we take a fall, youah a dead man. Hah-ley's kind of a lonah, but I got friends all ovuh."

Bradford felt something hard behind his right ear.

"Do. You. Understand?"

Bradford counted five seconds. "I understand."

"Don't spook him. He'll come through."

"One an' only time I work with 'im."

"Jesus, Bob!" Briscoe exclaimed. "What's the problem?"

"Reminds me of louies. Offisuhs an' gennulmen. Ninety percent of 'em are stupid, unlucky, or scared shitless."

Of course, thought Bradford. At Briscoe's place the old fart had been irony incarnate. A little booze and it went right by you. You stupid fuck.

"Gee, Bob," he said at last, "I thought we were pals."

"You did, didn't you? Cunt!"

"Come on, you guys! Knock it off!"

"What's that?"

"Cunt. Pussy. Gash. Cooze. Twat."

Bradford felt grateful. This was better than slapping helmets. He would kill this old man.

"Well, Harley. At least you know you're not the only one."

Silence.

Then, "What did you tell him?"

"Nothing. Just what you said about me and my wife."

"You talk too much."

"Cool off. Next light, we synchronize watches."

213

When they did so, Bradford noticed that his tremor was gone. Again he looked for Kaufman's people but did not see them His mind seemed clear Everywhere else he felt a bit numb, and his hands were dry. He wondered if he could be in shock.

When they crossed Fillmore Briscoe said, "This is fantastic. We're gonna be famous."

Bradford was breathing deep, counting respirations. Five a minute.

"Hey, Mickey. You know a big fat nigger named Morrell?"

"Yeah."

"He's the one who signed my kid's rejection letter, and he's on the program too. How's that for luck?"

By then Bradford knew what he had to do, and he was watching the line of parked cars on his right. Solid from corner to corner, it presented no opportunities.

Going to work, he drove this stretch every day, from Divisadero to Masonic, and never noticed a damned thing. But it did not take long to see what was required. There was one at the northwest corner of nearly every intersection. Some were solid stone, others hollow but made of iron. Either should do.

Near Central he slowed to a stop behind a line of cars. When the light changed and they began to move, he slowly let out the clutch without pressing the accelerator. The van jerked as the engine died.

"What the fuck?"

"Killed it," said Bradford.

Bradford depressed the clutch, turned the key, and the engine caught. He let out the clutch and the engine died again.

"Cunt can't even drive!"

"For Chrissake, give it some gas."

214

The engine roared. Bradford cleared the intersection as the light went yellow. Sped up. He was nearly to Masonic before they knew something was wrong.

"Slow down, Asshole!"

The light went yellow.

"Mickey—"

"SLOW DOWN!"

When Bradford leaned on the horn he expected a bullet, but it did not come. The left front tire blew when it hit the curb, and the truck began its flip an instant before they hit the pole.

TWENTY

Two days later in City and County Hospital, Bradford awoke just before dawn to see the face of Cheryl Kaufman. In the darkness it seemed suspended. Disembodied.

"Jesus!"

"Sorry. Didn't mean to scare you."

"The ghost of Christmas Future."

"All us spooks look alike."

"Oh. Very good."

"How you doin?"

"Could be worse." He was sleepy, sedated. His right leg was in a cast. It hurt and so did his ribs.

"Yes. It could."

"What happened to them?"

"Briscoe has a broken arm and jaw, also a concussion. Crawford has fractured vertabrae."

"I thought I might have killed Briscoe."

"Close. No cigar."

Bradford waited. He could see all of her now. Dark suit, blouse, tights. Navy blues.

"You did it on purpose."

"Yeah."

"Why?"

"Wal, it seemed like a good idea at the time."

"John Wayne. My hero."

"They were going to hit the Forum at Hamilton."

She nodded. "The moment you crashed, a colleague of mine was on the air with that possibility."

"Then you were following."

"Chasing is more like it. Three vehicles left that garage at about the same time. It took a while to be sure which was yours, and we were spread real thin. If they'd got inside the building, it could have been pretty nasty."

She brought a chair from a corner, sat beside him. He could smell cologne. Watch the skirt slide above her knees. He told her everything, beginning with Briscoe's arrival that morning. When he had finished, her face was still and thoughtful, her face clearer in the growing light, like a woman in a moody painting. Kurtz's Intended. Suddenly she tapped her thighs with her fingertips, *pit-pat*, near the hem of her skirt.

"Wish we'd had the wire on you."

"How could you have known?"

"Switches like that aren't unprecedented. But they spent so much time checking out Fernandez and the others, it just didn't seem likely. And like I said, we were spread thin."

"I gather there are problems."

"Yes."

"Such as."

"At the moment we can't talk to Briscoe. His jaw's all wired up, and he's intubated. But Crawford swears you were on your way to the gun range."

"A likely story. As they say."

"Yeah. But he and Briscoe've been there every Saturday this month. The range people confirm it."

"After the shootings, that's where they would have gone."

She nodded, turned her head to look at him. "In the van the only loaded gun was yours. They had Glocks, but empty and in cases. Clips in a bag."

"Entirely legal."

"Yes."

"How does he explain switching vehicles?"

"He claims you said the van was yours. And that Briscoe left his car because he had errands to run downtown later."

"Innocent as lambs."

"He said they'd been trying to keep you out of trouble since the business of Shapley's car. And that you were the one hot to blow people away."

"Uh-huh."

"What did they tell you about the van?"

"Nothing. We drove into the garage and there it was. Whose is it?"

"Nobody's. Somebody with fake ID bought it with cash from a dealer in San Mateo. And it wasn't one of our three guys."

"No?"

"We showed pictures to the dealer. He says it was somebody short, fat, and bald. That ring any bells?"

"No."

She nodded.

"And there's nothing else?"

"We've pretty much stripped their places, and there's stuff we have to check out. But right now none of it looks real promising."

"What about the paper trail?"

"The poster is a plus, but the threat it makes is a little vague. We can't prove these guys had anything to do with

218

what you got in the mail. It's generic, produced in the same plant in the Midwest. It's appeared all over the country."

"So. There's no case."

"We're not sure. We have the observations of our field people. We have the earlier tapes, which are suspicious but not conclusive. We have the funny business with the van. We have the poster. And we have Wilson."

"He talking?"

"Not yet. But he had a little dope and some stolen credit cards."

"Bargaining chips."

"Maybe. But right now he's stonewalling."

"You also have me."

"I was just coming to that."

"Tell me."

"The business of Shapley's car will compromise you, of course."

"Of course."

"On the other hand, Briscoe and Crawford have no felony convictions."

Bradford nodded.

Again Kaufman turned her rich eyes upon him. He imagined the contrast, pale man and dark woman in the whiteness. Edward Hopper.

"Something else."

"Which is."

"What is your relationship with Molly Marcus?"

"She's my illegitimate daughter."

Kaufman shook her head.

"Girlfriend."

"Ohhh."

Cheryl Kaufman closed her eyes.

"God damn you, Mickey."

"Sorry."

"Why didn't you tell me?"

219

"I wanted to keep her out of it."

"You fool." She covered the lower part of his face with her fingers.

"I'm sorry. I release you from our agreement. Feel free to prosecute on every count."

Her hand fell into her lap. "We may very well."

There was a long silence. At last she said, "An alcoholic teacher who screws his students and blows up cars is not exactly an unimpeachable witness."

"I guess not."

She got up, went slowly to the window, stood looking out. Perhaps two minutes passed. Then she looked down at him. Sternly.

"You know where my boss is?"

"The bald guy?"

"Yes. Alta Bates Hospital. His ulcer blew up. He thinks his career is over."

"Because he dealt with me."

"Partly. Our not getting you wired makes it worse."

"What will they do to you?"

"I think this time next year I'll be living with my mom and prepping for the bar."

"I'm sorry."

"To be honest, I was considering it anyway."

Bradford said nothing.

"It's not hopeless. Anything could happen."

"But it doesn't look good."

"No."

"How did you find Molly?"

"We found her finding you."

"Shit. She came to the hospital?"

"You never thought of that?"

"Crashing the van was spur of the moment. She told you about us?"

"No. Not even when I cornered her. She's very loyal to you."

"Cornered her how?"

"I recognized her voice."

"From the tape."

"Yes."

"Will she have to testify?"

"If there's a trial."

"Who else knows about her?"

"I advised her to tell her parents and bring them to see me. But for all I know, they're downtown right now, pressing charges against you."

"Fine."

Kaufman picked up her purse. "I've gotta go."

"Okay."

"Are you in pain?"

"A little."

"I'll tell the nurse."

"I think they've given me everything they can."

"I'm sorry, Mickey. I'm kind of afraid you're going to jail."

He nodded.

TWENTY-ONE

Soon after Bradford's talk with Cheryl Kaufman, his physicians cut back on his medication, and for two months thereafter he had pain in varying degrees. He kept an accounting of it, as if it were income. When his compound fracture was described to him, he troubled himself to envision it in detail: the broken stalks of bone protruding bloodily through his skin, the twist of the limb before it was reset, the skin soapy white or morbid purple under the cast. When they told him that the leg might be shorter than its mate, he thought of a profound limp, a constant backache, recurrent pain in the leg itself, a permanent grim set to his face. In his small way he would be Ahab, Ethan Frome.

It was not long before these imaginings, and even the memory of them, disgusted him.

Briscoe, Wilson, and Big Bob Crawford were arrested for conspiracy to commit murder, but three weeks later the charges were dropped. Briscoe and Crawford were released from jail. New charges of possession of marijuana and stolen credit cards were filed against Wynn Wilson; he was convicted and served six months of a one-year term in in the county jail. Soon after leaving the hospital Bradford himself went to court on crutches and pled guilty to three misdemeanor counts, destruction of property, carrying a concealed weapon, and reckless driving. Molly's name never came up. Bradford received two years' probation, on the condition that he quit drinking and make restitution to Bob Shapley. The school district instituted dismissal proceedings, and the state moved to revoke his teaching and administrative credentials.

A week after he left the hospital Molly called him at home. She questioned him about his injuries and the charges against him, speaking, he thought, a little faster than usual. He told her he was healing well and would not go to jail for blowing the car or crashing the van.

"Then you're home free," she said. "Because my parents won't press charges."

"That's pretty generous of them."

"Well--I told them I wouldn't testify. My father wants to punch you in the nose."

"I guess he's entitled."

"He's not going to. But look. To get them to chill, I had to promise something."

"I can guess what that is."

"I agreed to six months."

"Uh-huh."

"I'm being shipped to Europe for the summer. I'm not sure whether it's punishment or a graduation present."

"Maybe both."

"Are you angry?"

"No."

"Are you going to be madly, suicidally depressed?

"No."

"Well?"

"I'm not happy about it."

"Neither am I."

"Okay."

"If we're desperately, passionately, and eternally in love, six months shouldn't matter, right?"

"Right."

"And I'll be here in six months. I'm going to Stanford, not one of the Ivies."

"Congratulations."

"So we can get together,"

"Sure."

"Okay. Listen. They're downstairs, and I promised I'd keep this short."

"I understand."

"So this is goodbye for a while."

"Yes. By the way. Happy birthday."

Molly was silent.

"I can't do it."

"I know. You're right not to."

"What if it is a mistake?" She was crying now.

"It could be."

"Then why did you say that?"

"I apologize."

"Sometimes I think you are a bastard!"

"The evidence mounts."

"I'll call you in the fall, Mickey."

"Yes."

Two nights later the phone rang again.

"Hello?"

"Better get your ducks in a row, Bradford. You won't be around much longer."

"Took you long enough. I've been home for days."

The caller hung up. His voice was not familiar. *Ducks in a row*. An odd expression, thought Bradford, for guys like these.

The next night, as he washed his dishes, he heard an explosion in the distance, followed by what sounded like the skittering of mice in the kitchen wall. Bradford turned and saw the shiny, crystallized edges of a bullet hole in the largest window. He hit the deck, then reached for the wall switch and turned out the light. He lay still for several minutes. Then he opened the fridge, quickly pressing the little button to extinguish the light. He felt around for a Clausthaler and found it. Drank it in the dark, his back against the kitchen counter, wishing he had a real beer.

Eventually he called Cheryl Kaufman, and a half hour later she was there, accompanied by a young man in a dark suit, white shirt, and dark tie. He reminded Bradford of those nice Mormon boys who proselytize at bus stops.

They shook hands. "Are you her chaperon?"

Cheryl Kaufman shook her head. "Not funny."

While her colleague dug out the bullet, Bradford heard the skittering again. The dust of plaster, falling within the wall. Kaufman told him to stay home and keep his shades drawn.

"How close was it?"

"Missed by a mile."

"We'll reactivate the phone tap. Call the locals and keep an eye on you for a few days. But after that you'll be on your own. Unless they try again."

"Uh-huh."

"As rub-out attempts go, this one looks pretty half-assed. The bullet had to have been nearly spent."

"I was going to say."

"My guess is, they don't have the motivation for anything serious. But you never know."

Bradford nodded.

"Anything at all suspicious, you call us."

"Sure. By the way, how've you been?"

She frowned slightly. "How've I been."

"Yeah. I have a personal interest in your welfare."

"Mickey."

"I'm serious. Are they gonna fire you?"

"Maybe not. We're blaming everything on you."

When Kaufman and her partner left, Bradford retrieved loose cartridges from the basement drawer, went upstairs, and reloaded his father's .38. He put it into the bedside drawer, and his hands forgot to sweat.

For quite some time there were no calls, bullets, or other untoward events. Bradford remained on sick leave for another month, after which he received a letter from the district--it gave him a good laugh--saying that he would be on paid administrative leave until the end of the semester.

Soon he felt that the worst, aside from the loss of Molly, was over. He had his health, his house, his freedom. Though he was not sure why, he could not quite believe that people in the Movement would succeed in harming him. In early May the Board of Education directed the Superintendent to keep Hamilton open. Official explanations of this change in policy were unconvincing. Janie heard several rumors. One was that out-of-town alumni had brought pressure mysterious in nature. Another was that Freddy Lamar had lobbied for the school. His wife was a Hamilton graduate, as well as two of his major campaign contributors.

Bradford, who had stopped reading the newspapers, learned all of this during an after-school visit. Janie brought home-made chocolate chip cookies, and they sat at his kitchen table, munching and drinking coffee. She told him that John Rohrer had lost most of the sight in one eye. Around school, when he passed things on his left, he tended to bump into them.

At Bradford's request Janie had checked the district's attendance records for information on Rickey Bradford.

The boy had spent the remainder of the fall at the ranch and was now going to Lincoln High.

"Why did you want to know?"

"His P.O. asked if I thought the kid deserved a break. I waffled."

"But you're glad he got one."

"Seems only fair. I did."

"Yes."

Suddenly Bradford remembered to ask about the Forum.

"You don't know?"

"No. That was—"

"—Oh, of course! The day you were hurt!"

"Yeah."

"It was quite a scene. Rwanda made a rambling speech attacking the school and everybody in it. Then two kids from Alice's junior honors class got up and said they'd seen her let the air out of your tires on over-the-counter day, when she was out front waiting for Gordon to bring his car around. Rwanda started screaming at them, and when the Superintendent tried to calm her down, she nearly pushed him off the stage."

"Wonderful."

"Frankly, I felt sorry for both of them."

"You would."

"Do you still hate her?"

"I don't know. Mostly I see her as a sort of impersonal pestilence. Like a swarm of mosquitoes."

"I think she's tormented."

"I have trouble imagining that."

"Try."

Bradford's ribs healed quickly, his leg slowly. In June his doctor told him that in fact it was now shorter than its mate and that he would have a limp. Notwithstanding his earlier fantasies of disability, the news came as a shock. His response was to join a gym and spend hours a day in the weight room. He regained nine pounds he had lost and put on ten more. He cultivated a bit of a gut because he could not bear to look like a bodybuilder. By mid-August he could bench press three hundred and fifty pounds. In that same month his attorney struck a deal with the school district and the state. Bradford resigned; and, as *quid pro quo*, the state abandoned its effort to revoke his credentials. A week later Bradford went to work as a property manager for Tom Halliday's real estate firm.

Despite his new endeavors Bradford had long, empty hours. He went to bookstores with no idea of what he wanted to read, came home with nothing. He took long walks and ended up in stores where he bought items he did not require and, he would know the next day, did not even want. He subscribed to magazines he did not read. He played solitaire. He watched entire baseball games on TV, feeling spoiled and wasted when they were over, almost hung-over. He began projects on the house, some of them quite eccentric, such as the erection of a flagpole in the backyard. None were completed. In a notebook he sometimes made schedules for the days to follow, as if to convince himself that he had, if not a full life, at least a life. He kept himself sober, though AA meetings--which the court required him to attend--were not much help. People told their sad, humiliating stories, yet were remote. They seemed to regard one another as damaged goods.

He did his new work competently but did not particularly enjoy it. He had of course understood that his connections with owners, tenants, and handymen would not be profound. He recalled how he and his Hamilton colleagues had regularly made jokes about school not being the real world. Remembered, it now seemed far more more real than the so-called private sector. One night in late August he tried to call Molly but got only the answering machine, to which he did not respond. Bradford regretted visiting upon her a kind of grief which she should have been spared for five or ten more years. This regret was ironic and had no moral value, since he hoped to resume what they had had. There was no point in kidding himself about that.

With the check paying Bob Shapley for his car, Bradford included a letter of apology which expressed his hope that whatever anguish he had caused would pass with time. Bradford knew he deserved no reply but hoped for one anyway and, to his surprise, got it.

> Dear Mr. Bradford,
>
> Time I unfortunately do not have.
> I am dying of AIDS. But I will bear
> no grudges to the grave. I forgive
> everything and everyone.
>
> Sincerely,
> Bob Shapley

Several days later a pipe bomb exploded on Bradford's front porch at three in the morning. It shredded the rubber doormat, seared the door, and broke a window. Bradford surveyed the damage and went back to bed. In the morning he called Cheryl Kaufman.

She was there a half-hour later, wearing a red windbreaker and black tights.

"Why didn't you call when it happened?"

"Didn't want to get you out of bed."

She squatted down, ran her fingertip over an edge of the sooty burn. She put her fingertip to her tongue, then sniffed the blackened surface.

"More amateur stuff, huh?"

229

She nodded. "Wouldn't even have taken your leg off."

"Aw."

"Any warning? Phone calls?"

"Not this time."

"What's that in your pocket?"

"My father's .38."

"I thought you'd had enough of guns."

"Look. I'm a criminal. I'm a jerk. But I don't want to die, and I'm going to take care of myself."

"Don't ever take it out of the house."

Bradford did not reply.

"Second time around it's a felony. And you've got the only probation you're ever going to get."

"Are you gonna protect me from these guys, Cheryl?"

"We'll do what we did last time. But we can't provide twenty-four-hour guard."

Bradford gazed at her.

"Why don't you move out for a while? Get yourself a room someplace."

"And have 'em burn the place down when I'm not here? No way. I've lived here all my life."

In the kitchen he made coffee for them. She told him that Big Bob Crawford had suffered a stroke and was dying in the Veterans' home in Yountville. Wilson had completed his sentence, and Briscoe had sold his house. Both had disappeared.

"How many of those guys are out there?" asked Bradford.

"Lots. And they're getting smarter."

"Briscoe was pretty smart, huh?"

"Absolutely."

In September, on an impulse, Bradford signed up for night classes in law. He couldn't seem to stay away from schools. A month later Molly called. Again she was rather

230

brisk, and Bradford sensed that he was unfinished business. They agreed to meet for dinner in Palo Alto. For the occasion he got a haircut, had the car washed, and bought some new clothes. He had become too fat for his pallbearer's suit.

He offered to pick her up at the dorm, but she wanted to meet him at the restaurant. The significance of this seemed obvious, but he tried not to dwell upon it.

The restaurant was a large, elegant Colonial house of glistening white clapboard and green trim. He waited for her on its porch in poignant autumn twilight. She was ten minutes late when he saw her coming, head down, walking fast, dolly hair streaming. She wore jeans, running shoes, and a red Stanford sweatshirt. As she crossed the street the last of the sunset made her hair a burning mist, and he was suddenly aware of some change, some difference. When she had climbed the steps and stood before him, she bent slightly and kissed him on the cheek. He looked up at her, still and stunned. She had grown two inches.

"Good God."

She took his arm, gently turned him toward the oaken doors of the restaurant. "It started in the spring," she said. "You just didn't notice."

The restaurant had deep blond carpets, pale oak every where, fine linens, and not much of the college town about it, except parents dressed up, students down.

When they were seated, Bradford stared at her over his menu.

"Maybe you'll never stop. I can see it now, NCAA Finals, March 1999. The Attack of the Fifty-foot Low Post Player."

"Don't be cruel." She was studying her menu. "But it's incredible the difference it makes. On the court, I mean."

"Really."

231

She did not look up. "Really. Coach says without it I wouldn't get many minutes."

"And you seem . . . leaner."

"It's the program. We weigh in every Monday, and they don't let you get away with anything."

"That bother you?"

"Not much."

They waiter came, and they ordered. When he had gone, she said, "You know what? You look bigger too."

"Fatter."

"You're doing weights."

"How'd you know?"

"There's a look you get. Everybody here pumps iron. The jocks, that is."

"I'm developing a gut."

She shrugged. "You're a football player. You should see ours."

"Oh."

"What you realize, when you get into this, is that you'll have to work out for the rest of your <u>life</u>. If you don't, you'll be fat by thirty and dead by fifty."

"They teach you that?"

"Yeah."

She asked what he was doing. He had rehearsed two short paragraphs.

"Law school's a great idea, Mickey. You're just the type."

"It's just an experiment."

"No. It's <u>you</u>. You gotta do it."

Bradford laughed.

"You're a doer, like me. It's partly what got us together, I think."

Bradford was in no mood for suspense. "So. What do you think? Can we see each other?"

She was buttering bread, and her expression did not change. At last she said, "If you want. As an experiment."

Again he laughed.

She took his hand but still did not look up. "I'm different, Mickey. This summer I got Euro-pized. Now I'm getting Stanfordized."

"Is that where they keep you from shrinking?"

"What?"

"Nothing."

"I'm not saying it's all wonderful. It's a very intense, weird place. For jocks, at least. But I'm kind of buying into it."

"No point in being here if you don't."

"Actually, it's not just the jock scene. The academics too. I'm gonna try for a Rhodes."

"Good."

"When the basketball's over, I'll just be this six-two geek. I have to have other ways of getting respect."

"Wow. You are buying in."

"I don't get it."

"'Getting respect.' Only jocks talk like that."

"Oh." She looked annoyed. When the waiter removed the soup dishes, she asked, "How're you gonna feel being out with somebody taller than you?"

"I'll handle it."

"Yeah, well, it's gonna take some doing. I could see that in your face."

"I feel exactly as I did a year ago. I would marry you tonight."

"I'm not marrying anybody. Not for quite a while."

"That's okay too."

She did not reply.

The waiter brought their entrees.

"You don't think it's a good idea."

"What?"

233

"Our seeing each other."

"It's okay. As an experiment."

"I detect little enthusiasm."

"Well. It makes me nervous."

"I won't push. Promise."

"You were born pushing. Like me."

"How about this: dinner once in a while."

"Maybe that would be better."

"Okay."

In perhaps twenty seconds, Molly stopped eating, set down her fork. Her voice was steady.

"What's worse, Mickey? Me being a traitor, or us being miserable down the road?"

"You're not a traitor."

With the heel of one hand Molly struck the table, <u>thump</u>. A tear escaped, caught its breath on her cheek.

"<u>Answer the question!</u>"

He did, like a schoolboy reciting, bad grammar and all.

"Us being miserable down the road."

When he dropped her at the dorm, he asked, "You think you're going to regret this? Our . . . thing?"

"I don't know. Sometimes . . . "

"What?"

"Sometimes, when I'm with the people here, I feel like I'm watching a movie I've already seen the end of."

"Uh-huh."

"Do you understand what I mean?"

"Yes."

Driving home, Bradford again thought about suicide. He almost hoped that he would feel differently about it, but by the time he got home, he knew he did not. In the garage he sat still in the car.

"Square one," he said aloud.

But he knew it wasn't true. It was a new game, like it or not.

Ten days later, on a Sunday afternoon late in October, Bradford's doorbell rang. He went to the darkened living room and peered through a tiny, neat hole Kaufman had made in one blind. The figure he saw was at first entirely unfamiliar: a tall man in a stylish tweed jacket and cap, beige turtle-neck, and brown slacks. The brim of the cap cast a slight shadow on the upper half of his face, and the light of gray afternoon was not strong, and so Bradford squinted for several seconds before he recognized the Colonel, whom he had never before seen in anything but suit and tie. Bradford stepped back and was still a moment, deciding whether to go to the door.

But he did, and led the old man into the den. The Colonel took a hard straight chair, an antique. Bradford perched on the edge of the recliner.

"I considered coming sooner. Then decided to wait till things calmed down."

"Good idea."

"How is your leg?"

"Ninety percent of what it was. As good as it's going to get, probably."

"I was a bit surprised that you resigned."

"No point in staying, even if I'd won. They'd have stuck me in an office at 135 or Parkside, made me shuffle papers for twenty-five years."

"I hear you're working for Tom Halliday."

"Yes."

"I need to ask you a couple of things."

"Sure."

"I have thought a good deal about our conversations of last fall, and I have concluded that although I intended to be entirely non-directive, I probably was not. I must have encouraged you, at least implicitly, to get involved with those people. I wonder about the extent of my influence."

Bradford smiled. "Oh . . . I'd say it was a factor of three to five percent."

"And the larger causes were . . . "

"Seventy percent anger, abetted by booze. Twenty-five percent belief."

"Belief in what?"

Bradford thought about it. "Belief that the liberals and the mau-maus were screwing us over."

"If you yourself hadn't been victimized, you'd have done nothing."

"Right. I'm not real political. You know that."

"When you decided to become an informant, had your beliefs changed?"

"Not much. I still believe most of what I believed a year ago."

"Except?"

"Except the idea that any of it is worth killing people for."

"What is 'it'?"

"Everything they've done so far."

"I see. What would they have to do to cross the line?"

"Bomb Pearl harbor. Figuratively speaking. Kill and maim us good guys."

"A year ago you thought they had already crossed the line."

"Yeah."

"What changed your mind?"

"Seeing the elephant. As they say."

"That's a bit cryptic."

"What happened to Rohrer. And to an old black guy we nearly ran down."

"Rohrer is a soldier of the enemy. The old man would have been a regrettable civilian casualty. So you're saying that you would fight no war because of the inevitable killing."

"No. Just that the present stakes aren't high enough."

"I see."

The Colonel suddenly leaned forward, clasped his hands, rested his forearms on his knees. He did not look at Bradford and was silent for a few seconds.

"My second question is this. When you came to see me that last day, were you trying to get me to implicate myself? At the behest of your new FBI friends?"

"No. I did want to know if you were involved. But, as you'll recall, I never got around to asking."

"Why did you want to know?"

"By then I knew I'd been a fool. I was afraid you might have been too."

"If I had answered in the affirmative, what would you have done?"

"There was nothing I could have done. I just wanted to know. It was entirely personal."

"I don't understand."

"I've always admired you. I wanted to be convinced you weren't one of them. It would have made going into that weekend a little easier."

"But you were not convinced."

"I had no idea either way. You play it pretty close to the vest."

"I find it hard to believe that you wouldn't have informed on me. You informed on the others."

"Just between the two of us, Colonel. Off the record. Were you involved?"

The old man stood up. "I do not believe that I shall say."

"All right."

"Whether I was or not, you are an informer. A stool pigeon. You do not deserve the satisfaction of an answer."

"Up to you." Bradford rose, met the Colonel's gaze.

"When you choose to go to war, you cannot turn back."

"Oh yes you can. Lots of precedent there."

"There is always precedence for cowardice."

"That's true as well."

"Have you considered the possibility? That you are simply a coward?"

"Yes."

"And decided that you are not."

"Yes."

"Well. Thank you for answering my questions."

"No problem."

Bradford ate most of his meals out, studied in his free hours, and walked everywhere he could in order to stay in some kind of shape. He thought as little about the recent past as possible. In this he was fairly successful. Only once or twice a day did he think of Molly, or his old job, or the fact that he had once considered himself a better man than most. Rather more often he was troubled by all that he did not know about Briscoe, Crawford, Hensley, and their numberless allies in deed and spirit.

But if he was not happy, neither was he depressed. Bradford was much better at living in the moment than most people.

Law School was a private and unaccredited institution located near the foot of Haight Street, just over a mile from the house. He walked to and from class four nights a week, carrying his books in a backpack. He made acquaintances in his classes and enjoyed shooting the breeze during breaks. He even flirted with one of the women, a pretty blonde, though he did not ask her out. On his way home he often stopped at Church Street Station for hot chocolate and a croissant because he now slept better with a little something on his stomach. Then, heading up the last stretch of Market Street, he would see himself reflected in store windows and think that he looked much as he had in college.

On a cold, clear night in November he climbed the States Street hill, feeling pleasantly tired. Class had been more interesting than usual, and on the break the blonde had invited him to brunch at her place on Sunday. He had made excuses but come away pleased that he had been asked. From Corona Heights the smell of licorice was strong, a scent from childhood, his equivalent of the taste of Madeleine. He remembered the dry golden grass in which he and Lou Fanelli had played catch, the view of the city from Red Rock, and the solitary prowls through trees and brush on which he had hoped to come miraculously upon a loose and reckless female.

He had reached his front porch when someone called him by his last name. He turned and saw the form, melding into the dark steps and railing below. A small man in a baseball cap, his arm extended. Bradford thought of turning, putting the backpack between himself and the bullets, but the man fired twice before he could move.

Bradford's legs gave way, and then he was sitting down. The weight of the pack was about to pull him over backward and so he leaned forward a bit. The bullets had struck him in the chest, but now he felt nothing. The man ran away, down States Street.

Gunny, the beautiful man from the gun show.

Bradford did not know why he thought so. More likely Wilson. Bradford heard a car door slam, a car start up and roar away. He had walked right by them.

Then silence. The weapon had been of small caliber, the reports quick and not very loud, and now there was no movement anywhere. Apparently no one had noticed. Perfectly understandable.

Small caliber. The fact made him hopeful, but then he put his hand inside his jacket, felt the pulsing rush of blood. Not good.

Of course. He had thought he was getting off easy. Should have known better.

He noticed that he could still smell the licorice, but as soon as the fact registered, the scent began to fade. The darkness deepened. Someone came up the steps.

The terror began to rise, but Bradford shouted it down.

"Everybody does it," he cried. "Everybody!"

Tom Halliday kneeled beside him.

"What, Mickey?"

"Everybody does it, Tom!"

"Does what?"

He could not quite say it.

"You know."